The
Courts of Chaos

The
Courts of Chaos

ROGER ZELAZNY

DOUBLEDAY & COMPANY, INC.
GARDEN CITY, NEW YORK
1978

All of the characters in the book
are fictitious, and any resemblance
to actual persons, living or dead,
is purely coincidental.

THE COURTS OF CHAOS was originally serialized
in *Galaxy* magazine, November 1977 to February 1978.

Library of Congress Cataloging in Publication Data

Zelazny, Roger.
   The courts of chaos.

   I. Title.
PZ4.Z456Co   [PS3576.E43]   813'.5'4

ISBN: 0-385-13685-4
Library of Congress Catalog Card Number 78-3263

To Carl Yoke, First Reader——

From Lucetania to Euclid Park,
Sarcobatus Flats to Cygnus X-1——
May you live another ten thousand years.
May your lair be safe from trendeltiles.
May the diminutive deities
break their collective leg.

The
Courts of Chaos

Amber: high and bright atop Kolvir in the middle of the day. A black road: low and sinister through Garnath from Chaos to the south. Me: cursing, pacing and occasionally reading in the library of the palace in Amber. The door to that library: closed and barred.

The mad prince of Amber seated himself at the desk, returned his attention to the opened volume. There was a knock on the door.

"Go away!" I said.

"Corwin. It's me—Random. Open up, huh? I even brought lunch."

"Just a minute."

I got to my feet again, rounded the desk, crossed the room. Random nodded when I opened the door. He carried a tray, which he took to a small table near the desk.

"Plenty of food there," I said.

"I'm hungry, too."

"So do something about it."

He did. He carved. He passed me some meat on a slab of bread. He poured wine. We seated ourselves and ate.

"I know you are still mad . . ." he said, after a time.

"Aren't you?"

"Well, maybe I am more used to it. I don't know. Still . . . Yes. It was sort of abrupt, wasn't it?"

"Abrupt?" I took a large swallow of wine. "It is just

like the old days. Worse even. I had actually come to like him when he was playing at being Ganelon. Now that he is back in control he is just as peremptory as ever, he has given us a set of orders he has not bothered to explain and he has disappeared again."

"He said he would be in touch soon."

"I imagine he intended that last time, too."

"I'm not so sure."

"And he explained nothing about his other absence. In fact, he has not really explained anything."

"He must have his reasons."

"I am beginning to wonder, Random. Do you think his mind might finally be going?"

"He was still sharp enough to fool you."

"That was a combination of low animal cunning and shapeshifting ability."

"It worked, didn't it?"

"Yes. It worked."

"Corwin, could it be that you do not want him to have a plan that might be effective, that you do not want him to be right?"

"That is ridiculous. I want this mess cleared up as much as any of us."

"Yes, but wouldn't you rather the answer came from another quarter?"

"What are you getting at?"

"You do not want to trust him."

"I will admit that. I have not seen him—as himself—in a hell of a long time, and . . ."

He shook his head.

"That is not what I mean. You are angry that he is back, aren't you? You hoped that we had seen the last of him."

I looked away.

"There is that," I finally said. "But not for a vacant throne, or not *just* for it. It is him, Random. Him. That's all."

"I know," he said. "But you have to admit he suckered Brand, which is not an easy thing to do. He pulled a stunt I still do not understand, getting you to bring that arm back from Tir-na Nog'th, somehow getting me to pass it along to Benedict, seeing to it that Benedict was in the right place at the proper moment, so that everything worked and he got the Jewel back. He is also still better than we are at Shadow play. He managed it right on Kolvir when he took us to the primal Pattern. I cannot do that. Neither can you. And he was able to whip Gérard. I do not believe that he is slowing down. I think he knows exactly what he is doing, and whether we like it or not, I think he is the only one who can deal with the present situation."

"You are trying to say that I should trust him?"

"I am trying to say that you have no choice."

I sighed.

"I guess you've put your finger on it," I said. "No sense in my being bitter. Still . . ."

"The attack order bothers you, doesn't it?"

"Yes, among other things. If we would wait longer, Benedict could field a greater force. Three days is not much time to get ready for something like this. Not when we are so uncertain about the enemy."

"But we may not be. He spoke in private with Benedict for a long while."

"And that is the other thing. These separate orders. This secrecy . . . He is not trusting us any more than he has to."

Random chuckled. So did I.

"All right," I said. "Maybe I would not either. But three days to launch a war." I shook my head. "He had better know something we don't."

"I get the impression that it is more a peremptory strike than a war."

"Only he did not bother to tell us what we are preempting."

Random shrugged, poured more wine.

"Perhaps he will say when he gets back. You did not get any special orders, did you?"

"Just to stand and wait. What about you?"

He shook his head.

"He said that when the time comes, I will know. At least with Julian, he told him to have his troops ready to move on a moment's notice."

"Oh? Aren't they staying in Arden?"

He nodded.

"When did he say this?"

"After you left. He trumped Julian up here to give him the message, and they rode off together. I heard Dad say that he would ride partway back with him."

"Did they take the eastern trail over Kolvir?"

"Yes. I saw them off."

"Interesting. What else did I miss?"

He shifted in his seat.

"The part that bothers me," he said. "After Dad had mounted and waved a good-bye, he looked back at me and said, 'And keep an eye on Martin.'"

"That is all?"

"That is all. But he was laughing as he said it."

"Just natural suspicion at a newcomer, I guess."

"Then why the laugh?"

"I give up."

I cut a piece of cheese and ate it.

"Might not be a bad idea, though. It might not be suspicion. Maybe he feels Martin needs to be protected from something. Or both. Or neither. You know how he sometimes is."

Random stood.

"I had not thought through to the alternative. Come with me now, huh?" he said. "You have been up here all morning."

"All right." I got to my feet, buckled on Grayswandir. "Where is Martin, anyway?"

"I left him down on the first floor. He was talking with Gérard."

"He is in good hands, then. Is Gérard going to be staying here, or will he be returning to the fleet?"

"I do not know. He would not discuss his orders."

We left the room. We headed for the stairway.

On the way down, I heard some small commotion from below and I quickened my pace.

I looked over the railing and saw a throng of guards at the entrance to the throne room, along with the massive figure of Gérard. All of them had their backs to us. I leaped down the final stairs. Random was not far behind me.

I pushed my way through.

"Gérard, what is happening?" I asked.

"Damned if I know," he said. "Look for yourself. But there is no getting in."

He moved aside and I took a step forward. Then another. And that was it. It was as if I were pushing against a slightly resilient, totally invisible wall. Beyond was a sight that tied my memory and feelings into a knot. I stiffened, as fear took hold of me by the neck, clasped my hands. No mean trick, that.

Martin, smiling, still held a Trump in his left hand, and Benedict—apparently recently summoned—stood before him. A girl was nearby, on the dais, beside the throne, facing away. Both men appeared to be speaking, but I could not hear the words.

Finally, Benedict turned and seemed to address the girl. After a time, she appeared to be answering him. Martin moved off to her left. Benedict mounted the dais as she spoke. I could see her face then. The exchange continued.

"That girl looks somewhat familiar," said Gérard, who had moved forward and now stood at my side.

"You might have gotten a glimpse of her as she rode past us," I told him, "the day Eric died. It's Dara."

I heard his sudden intake of breath.

"Dara!" he said. "Then you . . ." His voice faded.

"I was not lying," I said. "She is real."

"Martin!" cried Random, who had moved up on my right. "Martin! What's going on!"

There was no response.

"I don't think he can hear you," Gérard said. "This barrier seems to have cut us off completely."

Random strained forward, his hands pushing against something unseen.

"Let's all of us give it a shove," he said.

So I tried again. Gérard also threw his weight against the invisible wall.

After half a minute without success, I eased back.

"No good," I said. "We can't move it."

"What is the damned thing?" Random asked. "What is holding—"

I'd had a hunch—only that, though—as to what might be going on. And only because of the *déjà vu* character of the entire piece. Now, though . . . Now I clasped my hand to my scabbard, to assure myself that Grayswandir still hung at my side.

It did.

Then how could I explain the presence of my distinctive blade, its elaborate tracery gleaming for all to see, hanging where it had suddenly appeared, without support, in the air before the throne, its point barely touching Dara's throat?

I could not.

But it was too similar to what had happened that night in the dream city in the sky, Tir-na Nog'th, to be a coincidence. Here were none of the trappings—the darkness, the confusion, the heavy shadows, the tumultuous emotions I had known—and yet the piece was set much as it had been that night. It was very similar. But not precisely so. Benedict's stance seemed somewhat off—farther back, his body angled differently. While I could not read her lips, I wondered whether Dara was asking the same strange questions. I doubted it. The tableau—like, yet unlike, that which I had experienced—had probably been colored at the other end—that is, if there were any connection at all—by the effects of Tir-na Nog'th's powers upon my mind at that time.

"Corwin," Random said, "that looks like Grayswandir hanging in front of her."

"It does, doesn't it?" I said. "But as you can see, I am wearing my blade."

"There can't be another just like it . . . can there? Do you know what is happening?"

"I am beginning to feel as if I may," I said. "Whatever, I am powerless to stop it."

Benedict's blade suddenly came free and engaged the other, so like my own. In a moment, he was fighting an invisible opponent.

"Give him hell, Benedict!" Random shouted.

"It is no use," I said. "He is about to be disarmed."

"How can you know?" Gérard asked.

"Somehow, that is me in there, fighting with him," I said. "This is the other end of my dream in Tir-na Nog'th. I do not know how he managed it, but this is the price for Dad's recovering the Jewel."

"I do not follow you," he said.

I shook my head.

"I do not pretend to understand how it is being done," I told him. "But we will not be able to enter until two things have vanished from that room."

"What two things?"

"Just watch."

Benedict's blade had changed hands, and his gleaming prosthesis shot forward and fixed itself upon some unseen target. The two blades parried one another, locked, pressed, their points moving toward the ceiling. Benedict's right hand continued to tighten.

Suddenly, the Grayswandir blade was free, and moving past the other. It struck a terrific blow to Benedict's right arm at the place where the metal portion joined it. Then Benedict turned and the action was blocked to our view for several moments.

Then the sight was clear again, as Benedict dropped to one knee, turning. He clutched at the stump of his arm. The mechanical hand/arm hung in the air near Grayswandir. It was moving away from Benedict and descending, as was the blade. When both reached the floor, they did not strike it but passed on through, vanishing from sight.

I lurched forward, recovered my balance, moved ahead. The barrier was gone.

Martin and Dara reached Benedict before we did. Dara had already torn a strip from her cloak and was binding Benedict's stump when Gérard, Random and I got there.

Random seized Martin by the shoulder and turned him.

"What happened?" he asked.

"Dara . . . Dara told me she wanted to see Amber," he said. "Since I live here now, I agreed to bring her through and show her around. Then—"

"Bring her through? You mean on a Trump?"

"Well, yes."

"Yours or hers?"

Martin raked his lower lip with his teeth.

"Well, you see . . ."

"Give me those cards," said Random, and he snatched the case from Martin's belt. He opened it and began going through them.

"Then I thought to tell Benedict, since he was interested in her," Martin went on. "Then Benedict wanted to come and see—"

"What the hell!" Random said. "There is one of you, one of her, and one of a guy I've never even seen before! Where did you get these?"

"Let me see them," I said.

He passed me the three cards.

"Well?" he said. "Was it Brand? He is the only one I know who can make Trumps now."

"I would not have anything to do with Brand," Martin replied, "except to kill him."

But I already knew they were not from Brand. They were simply not in his style. Nor were they in the style of anyone whose work I knew. Style was not foremost in my mind at that moment, however. Rather, it was the features of the third person, the one whom Random had said he had never seen before. I had. I was looking at the face of the youth who had confronted me with a crossbow before the Courts of Chaos, recognized me and then declined to shoot.

I extended the card.

"Martin, who is this?" I asked.

"The man who made these extra Trumps," he said. "He drew one of himself while he was about it. I do not know his name. He is a friend of Dara's."

"You are lying," Random said.

"Then let Dara tell us," I said, and I turned to her.

She still knelt beside Benedict, though she had finished bandaging him and he was now sitting up.

"How about it?" I said, waving the card at her. "Who is this man?"

She glanced at the card, then up at me. She smiled.

"You really do not know?" she said.

"Would I be asking if I did?"

"Then look at it again and go look in a mirror. He is your son as much as mine. His name is Merlin."

I am not easily shocked, but this had nothing of ease about it. I felt dizzy. But my mind moved quickly. With the proper time differential the thing was possible.

"Dara," I said, "what is it that you want?"

"I told you when I walked the Pattern," she said, "that Amber must be destroyed. What I want is to have my rightful part in it."

"You will have my old cell," I said. "No, the one next to it. Guards!"

"Corwin, it is all right," Benedict said, getting to his feet. "It is not as bad as it sounds. She can explain everything."

"Then let her start now."

"No. In private. Just family."

I motioned back the guards who had come at my call.

"Very well. Let us adjourn to one of the rooms up the hall."

He nodded, and Dara took hold of his left arm. Random, Gérard, Martin and I followed them out. I looked back once to the empty place where my dream had come true. Such is the stuff.

2

I rode up over the crest of Kolvir and dismounted when I came to my tomb. I went inside and opened the casket. It was empty. Good. I was beginning to wonder. I had half-expected to see myself laid out before me, evidence that despite signs and intuitions I had somehow wandered into the wrong shadow.

I went back outside and rubbed Star's nose. The sun was shining and the breeze was chill. I had a sudden desire to go to sea. I seated myself on the bench instead and fumbled with my pipe.

We had talked. Seated with her legs beneath her on the brown sofa, Dara had smiled and repeated the story of her descent from Benedict and Lintra, the hellmaid, growing up in and about the Courts of Chaos, a grossly non-Euclidean realm where time itself presented strange distribution problems.

"The things you told me when we met were lies," I said. "Why should I believe you now?"

She had smiled and regarded her fingernails.

"I had to lie to you then," she explained, "to get what I wanted from you."

"That being . . . ?"

"Knowledge, of the family, the Pattern, the Trumps, of Amber. To gain your trust. To have your child."

"The truth would not have served as well?"

"Hardly. I come from the enemy. My reasons for wanting these things were not the sort of which you would approve."

"Your swordplay . . . ? You told me then that Benedict had trained you."

She smiled again and her eyes showed dark fires.

"I learned from the great Duke Borel himself, a High Lord of Chaos."

". . . and your appearance," I said. "It was altered on a number of occasions when I saw you walk the Pattern. How? Also, why?"

"All whose origins involve Chaos are shapeshifters," she replied.

I thought of Dworkin's performance the night he had impersonated me.

Benedict nodded.

"Dad fooled us with his Ganelon disguise."

"Oberon is a son of Chaos," Dara said, "a rebel son of a rebel father. But the power is still there."

"Then why is it we cannot do it?" Random asked.

She shrugged.

"Have you ever tried? Perhaps you can. On the other hand, it may have died out with your generation. I do not know. As to myself, however, I have certain favored shapes to which I revert in times of stress. I grew up where this was the rule, where the other shape was actually sometimes dominant. It is still a reflex with me. This is what you witnessed—that day."

"Dara," I said, "why did you want the things that you said you wanted—knowledge of the family, the Pattern, the Trumps, Amber? And a son?"

"All right." She sighed. "All right. You are by now

aware of Brand's plans—the destruction and rebuilding of Amber. . . ?"

"Yes."

"This involved our consent and co-operation."

"Including the murder of Martin?" Random asked.

"No," she said. "We did not know who he intended to use as the—agent."

"Would it have stopped you had you known?"

"You are asking a hypothetical question," she said. "Answer it yourself. I am glad that Martin is still alive. That is all that I can say about it."

"All right," Random said. "What about Brand?"

"He was able to contact our leaders by methods he had learned from Dworkin. He had ambitions. He needed knowledge, power. He offered a deal."

"What sort of knowledge?"

"For one thing, he did not know how to destroy the Pattern—"

"Then you *were* responsible for what he did," Random said.

"If you choose to look at it that way."

"I do."

She shrugged, looked at me.

"Do you want to hear this story?"

"Go ahead." I glanced at Random and he nodded.

"Brand was given what he wanted," she said, "but he was not trusted. It was feared that once he possessed the power to shape the world as he would, he would not stop with ruling over a revised Amber. He would attempt to extend his dominion over Chaos as well. A weakened Amber was what was desired, so that Chaos would be stronger than it now is—the striking of a new balance, giving to us more of the shadowlands that lie between our realms. It was realized long ago that the two kingdoms can never be merged, or one destroyed, without also disrupting all the processes that lie in flux between us. Total stasis or complete chaos would be the result. Yet, though it was seen what Brand had in mind, our leaders came to terms with him. It was the best opportunity to present itself in ages. It had to be seized. It was felt that Brand could be dealt with, and finally replaced, when the time came."

"So you were also planning a double-cross," Random said.

"Not if he kept his word. But then, we knew that he would not. So we provided for the move against him."

"How?"

"He would be allowed to accomplish his end and then be destroyed. He would be succeeded by a member of the royal family of Amber who was also of the first family of the Courts, one who had been raised among us and trained for the position. Merlin even traces his connection with Amber on both sides, through my forebear Benedict and directly from yourself—the two most favored claimants to your throne."

"You are of the royal house of Chaos?"

She smiled.

I rose. Strode away. Stared at the ashes on the grate.

"I find it somewhat distressing to have been involved in a calculated breeding project," I said, at length. "But be that as it may, and accepting everything you have said as true—for the moment—why are you telling us all of these things now?"

"Because," she said, "I fear that the lords of my realm would go as far for their vision as Brand would for his. Farther, perhaps. That balance I spoke of. Few seem to appreciate what a delicate thing it is. I have traveled in the shadowlands near to Amber, and I have walked in Amber herself. I also have known the shadows that lie by Chaos' side. I have met many people and seen many things. Then, when I encountered Martin and spoke with him, I began to feel that the changes I had been told would be for the better would not simply result in a revision of Amber more along the lines of my elders' liking. They would, instead, turn Amber into a mere extension of the Courts, most of the shadows would boil away to join with Chaos. Amber would become an island. Some of my seniors who still smart at Dworkin's having created Amber in the first place are really seeking a return to the days before this happened. Total Chaos, from which all things arose. I see the present condition as superior and I wish to preserve it. My desire is that neither side emerge victorious in any conflict."

I turned in time to see Benedict shaking his head.

"Then you are on neither side," he stated.

"I like to think that I am on both."

"Martin," I said, "are you in this with her?"

He nodded.

Random laughed.

"The two of you? Against both Amber and the Courts of Chaos? What do you hope to achieve? How do you plan to further this notion of balance?"

"We are not alone," she said, "and the plan is not ours."

Her fingers dipped into her pocket. Something glittered when she withdrew them. She turned it in the light. It was our father's signet ring that she held.

"Where did you get that?" Random asked.

"Where else?"

Benedict stepped toward her and held out his hand. She gave it to him. He scrutinized it.

"It *is* his," he said. "It has the little markings on the back that I've seen before. Why do you have it?"

"First, to convince you that I am acting properly when I convey his orders," she said.

"How is it that you even know him?" I asked.

"I met him during his—difficulties—some time back," she told us. "In fact, you might say that I helped to deliver him from them. This was after I had met Martin, and I was inclined to be more sympathetic toward Amber. But then, your father is also a charming and persuasive man. I decided that I could not simply stand by and see him remain prisoner to my kin."

"Do you know how he was captured in the first place?"

She shook her head.

"I only know that Brand effected his presence in a shadow far enough from Amber that he could be taken there. I believe it involved a fake quest for a nonexistent magical tool which might heal the Pattern. He realizes now that only the Jewel can do it."

"Your helping him to get away . . . How did this affect your relations with your own people?"

"Not too damned well," she said. "I am temporarily without a home."

"And you want one here?"

She smiled again.

"It depends on how things turn out. If my people have their way, I would as soon go back—or stay with what shadows remain."

I withdrew a Trump, glanced at it.

"What of Merlin? Where is he now?"

"They have him," she said. "I fear he may be their man

now. He knows his parentage, but they have had charge of his education for a long while. I do not know whether he could be gotten away."

I raised the Trump, stared at it.

"No good," she said. "It will not function between here and there."

I recalled how difficult Trump communication had been when I had been to the fringes of that place. I tried anyway.

The card grew cold in my hand and I reached out. There was the faintest flicker of a responding presence. I tried harder.

"Merlin, this is Corwin," I said. "Do you hear me?"

I seemed to hear a reply. It seemed to be, "I cannot—" And then there was nothing. The card lost its coldness.

"Did you reach him?" she asked.

"I am not sure," I said. "But I think so. Just for a moment."

"Better than I thought," she said. "Either conditions are good or your minds are very similar."

"When you began waving Dad's signet around you spoke of orders," Random said. "What orders? And why is he sending them through you?"

"It is a matter of timing."

"Timing? Hell! He just left here this morning!"

"He had to finish one thing before he was ready for another. He had no idea how long it would take. But I was just in touch with him before I came here—though I was hardly prepared for the reception I walked into—and he is now ready to begin the next phase."

"Where did you speak with him?" I asked. "Where is he?"

"I have no idea where he is. He contacted me."

"And . . . ?"

"He wants Benedict to attack immediately."

Gérard finally stirred from the huge armchair in which he had sat listening. He rose to his feet, hooked his thumbs in his belt and looked down at her.

"An order like that would have to come directly from Dad."

"It did," she said.

He shook his head.

"It makes no sense. Why contact you—someone we have small reason to trust—rather than one of us?"

"I do not believe that he can reach you at the moment. On the other hand, he was able to reach me."

"Why?"

"He did not use a Trump. He does not have one for me. He used a reverberation effect of the black road, similar to the means by which Brand once escaped Corwin."

"You know a lot of what has been going on."

"I do. I still have sources in the Courts, and Brand transported himself there after your struggle. I hear things."

"Do you know where our father is right now?" Random asked.

"No, I do not know. But I believe that he has journeyed to the real Amber, to take counsel with Dworkin and to re-examine the damage to the primal Pattern."

"To what end?"

"I do not know. Probably to decide on the course of action he will take. The fact that he reached me and ordered the attack most likely means that he has decided."

"How long ago was this communication?"

"Just a few hours—my time. But I was far from here in

Shadow. I do not know what the time differential is. I am too new at this."

"So it could be something extremely recent. Possibly only moments ago," Gérard mused. "Why did he talk with you rather than one of us? I do not believe that he could not reach us if he wished to."

"Perhaps to show that he looks upon me with favor," she said.

"All of this may be entirely true," Benedict stated. "But I am not moving without a confirmation of that order."

"Is Fiona still at the primal Pattern?" Random asked.

"Last I heard," I told him, "she had set up camp there. I see what you mean. . . ."

I shuffled out Fi's card.

"It took more than one of us to get through from there," he observed.

"True. So give me a hand."

He rose, came to my side. Benedict and Gérard also approached.

"This is not really necessary," Dara protested.

I ignored her and concentrated on the delicate features of my red-haired sister. Moments later, we had contact.

"Fiona," I asked, seeing from the background that she was still in residence at the heart of things, "is Dad there?"

"Yes," she said, smiling tightly. "He is inside with Dworkin."

"Listen, urgency prevails. I do not know whether or not you know Dara, but she is here—"

"I know who she is, but I have never met her."

"Well, she claims she has an attack order for Benedict,

from Dad. She has his signet to back it up, but he did not speak of this earlier. Do you know anything about it?"

"No," she said. "All we did was exchange greetings when he and Dworkin were out here earlier to look at the Pattern. I had some suspicions then, though, and this confirms them."

"Suspicions? What do you mean?"

"I think Dad is going to try to repair the Pattern. He has the Jewel with him, and I overheard some of the things he said to Dworkin. If he makes the attempt, they will be aware of it in the Courts of Chaos the moment that he begins. They will try to stop him. He would want to strike first to keep them occupied. Only . . ."

"What?"

"It is going to kill him, Corwin. I know that much about it. Whether he succeeds or fails, he will be destroyed in the process."

"I find it hard to believe."

"That a king would give up his life for the realm?"

"That Dad would."

"Then either he has changed or you never really knew him. But I do believe he is going to try it."

"Then why send his latest order by someone he knows we do not really trust?"

"To show that he wants you to trust her, I would guess, once he has confirmed it."

"It seems a roundabout way of doing things, but I agree that we should not act without that confirmation. Can you get it for us?"

"I will try. I will get back to you as soon as I have spoken with him."

She broke the contact.

I turned toward Dara, who had heard only our side of the conversation.

"Do you know what Dad is going to do right now?" I asked her.

"Something involving the black road," she said. "He had indicated that much. What, though, or how, he did not say."

I turned away. I squared my cards and encased them. I did not like this turning of events. This entire day had started badly, and things had been going downhill ever since. It was only a little past lunchtime, too. I shook my head. When I had spoken with him, Dworkin had described the results of any attempt to repair the Pattern, and they had sounded pretty horrendous to me. Supposing Dad tried it, failed, and got himself killed in the attempt? Where would we be then? Right where we were now, only without a leader, on the eve of battle—and with the succession problem stirring again. That whole ghastly business would be in the back of our minds as we rode to the wars, and we would all begin our private arrangements to fight one another once more as soon as the current enemy was dealt with. There had to be another way of handling things. Better Dad alive and on the throne than a revival of the succession intrigues.

"What are we waiting for?" Dara asked. "Confirmation?"

"Yes," I replied.

Random began to pace. Benedict seated himself and tested the dressing on his arm. Gérard leaned against the mantelpiece. I stood and thought. An idea came to me just then. I pushed it away immediately, but it returned. I did not like it, but that had nothing to do with practicalities. I would have to move quickly, though, before I had a chance to talk myself around to another viewpoint. No. I would stick with this one. Damn it!

There came a stirring of contact. I waited. Moments later, I regarded Fiona again. She stood in a familiar place that it took me several seconds to recognize: Dworkin's sitting room, on the other side of the heavy door at the back of the cave. Dad and Dworkin were both with her. Dad had dropped his Ganelon disguise and was his old self once again. I saw that he wore the Jewel.

"Corwin," Fiona said, "it is true. Dad did send the attack order with Dara, and he expected this call for confirmation. I—"

"Fiona, bring me through."

"What?"

"You heard me. Now!"

I extended my right hand. She reached forward and we touched.

"Corwin!" Random shouted. "What's happening!"

Benedict was on his feet, Gérard already moving toward me.

"You will hear about it shortly," I said, and I stepped forward.

I squeezed her hand before I released it and I smiled.

"Thanks, Fi. Hello, Dad. Hi, Dworkin. How's everything?"

I glanced once at the heavy door, saw that it stood open. Then I passed around Fiona and moved toward them. Dad's head was lowered, his eyes narrowed. I knew that look.

"What is this, Corwin? You are here without leave," he said. "I have confirmed that damned order, now I expect it to be carried out."

"It will be," I said, nodding. "I did not come here to argue about that."

"What, then?"

I moved nearer, calculating my words as well as the distance. I was glad that he had remained seated.

"For a time we rode as comrades," I said. "Damned if I did not come to like you then. I never had before, you know. Never had guts enough to say that before either, but you know it is true. I like to think that that is how things could have been, if we had not been what we are to each other." For the barest moment, his gaze seemed to soften as I positioned myself. Then, "At any rate," I went on, "I am going to believe in you that way rather than this way, because there is something I would never have done for you otherwise."

"What?" he asked.

"This."

I seized the Jewel with an upward sweeping motion and snapped the chain up over his head. I pivoted on my heel then and raced across the room and through the door. I drew it shut behind me and snapped it to. I could see no way to bar it from the outside, so I ran on, retracing the route through the cave from that night I had followed Dworkin along it. Behind me, I heard the expected bellow.

I followed the twistings. I stumbled only once. Wixer's smell still hung heavy in his lair. I pounded on and a final turning brought me a view of daylight ahead.

I raced toward it, slipping the Jewel's chain over my head as I went. I felt it fall to my breast, I reached down into it with my mind. There were echoes in the cave behind me.

Outside!

I sprinted toward the Pattern, feeling through the Jewel, turning it into an extra sense. I was the only person other than Dad or Dworkin fully attuned to it. Dworkin had told me that the Pattern's repair might be effected by a person's walking the Grand Pattern in such a state of attunement, burning out the smear at each crossing, replacing it with stock from the image of the Pattern that he bore within him, wiping out the black road in the process. Better me than Dad, then. I still felt that the black road owed something of its final form to the strength my curse against Amber had given it. I wanted to wipe that out, too. Dad would do a better job of putting things together after the war than I ever could, anyway. I realized, at that moment, that I no longer wanted the throne. Even if it were available, the prospect of administering to the kingdom down all the dull centuries that might lie before me was overwhelming. Maybe I would be taking the easy way out if I died in this effort. Eric was dead, and I no longer hated him. The other thing that had driven me—the throne—seemed now to have been desirable only because I'd thought he had wanted it so. I renounced both. What was left? I had laughed at Vialle, then wondered. But she had been right. The old soldier in me was strongest. It was a matter of duty. But not duty alone. There was more. . . .

I reached the edge of the Pattern, quickly made my way toward its beginning. I glanced back at the cave-mouth. Dad, Dworkin, Fiona—none of them had yet emerged. Good. They could never make it in time to stop me. Once I set foot on the Pattern, it would be too late for them to do anything but wait and watch. I thought for a fleeting instant of Iago's dissolution, pushed that thought away, strove to calm my mind to the level necessary for the undertaking, recalled my battle with Brand in this place and his strange departure, pushed that away, too, slowed my breathing, prepared myself.

A certain lethargy came upon me. It was time to begin, but I held back for a moment, trying to fix my mind properly on the grand task that lay before me. The Pattern swam for a moment in my vision. Now! Damn it! Now! No more preliminaries! Begin, I told myself. Walk!

Still, I stood, contemplating the Pattern as in a dream. I forgot about myself for long moments as I regarded it. The Pattern, with its long black smear to be removed . . .

It no longer seemed important that it might kill me. My mind drifted, considering the beauty of the thing. . . .

I heard a sound. It would be Dad, Dworkin, Fiona, coming. I had to do something before they reached me. I had to walk it, in a moment. . . .

I pulled my gaze away from the Pattern and glanced back toward the cavemouth. They had emerged, come partway down the slope and halted. Why? Why had they stopped?

What did it matter? I had the time I needed in which to begin. I began to raise my foot, to step forward.

I could barely move. I inched my foot ahead with a great effort of will. Taking this first step was proving worse than walking the Pattern itself, near to the end. But it did not seem so much an external resistance I fought against as it did the sluggishness of my own body. It was almost as if—

Then I had me an image of Benedict beside the Pattern in Tir-na Nog'th, Brand approaching, mocking, the Jewel burning upon his breast.

Before I looked down, I knew what I would see.

The red stone was pulsing in time with my heartbeat.

Damn them!

Either Dad or Dworkin—or both of them—reached through it at this instant, paralyzing me. I did not doubt that either of them could manage it alone. Still, at this distance, it was not worth surrendering without a fight.

I continued to push forward with my foot, sliding it slowly ahead toward the edge of the Pattern. Once I made it, I did not see how they . . .

Drowsing . . . I felt myself beginning to fall. I had been asleep for a moment. It happened again.

When I opened my eyes, I could see a portion of the Pattern. When I turned my head, I saw feet. When I looked up, I saw Dad holding the Jewel.

"Go away," he said to Dworkin and Fiona, without turning his head toward them.

They withdrew as he placed the Jewel about his own neck. He leaned forward then and extended his hand. I took it and he drew me to my feet.

"That was a damfool thing to do," he said.

"I almost made it."

He nodded.

"Of course, you would have killed yourself and not ac- complished anything," he said. "But it was well done nev- ertheless. Come on, let's walk."

He took my arm, and we began to move about the pe- riphery of the Pattern.

I watched that strange sky-sea, horizonless about us, as we went. I wondered what would have happened had I been able to begin the Pattern, what would be happening at that moment.

"You have changed," he finally said, "or else I never re- ally knew you."

I shrugged.

"Something of both perhaps. I was about to say the same of you. Tell me something?"

"What?"

"How difficult was it for you, being Ganelon?"

He chuckled.

"Not hard at all," he said. "You may have had a glimpse of the real me."

"I liked him. Or, rather, you being him. I wonder whatever became of the real Ganelon?"

"Long dead, Corwin. I met him after you had exiled him from Avalon, long ago. He wasn't a bad chap. Wouldn't have trusted him worth a damn, but then I never trust anyone I don't have to."

"It runs in the family."

"I regretted having to kill him. Not that he gave me much choice. All this was very long ago, but I remembered him clearly, so he must have impressed me."

"And Lorraine?"

"The country? A good job, I thought. I worked the proper shadow. It grew in strength by my very presence, as any will if one of us stays around for long—as with you in Avalon, and later that other place. And I saw that I had a long while there by exercising my will upon its time-stream."

"I did not know that could be done."

"You grow in strength slowly, beginning with your initiation into the Pattern. There are many things you have yet to learn. Yes, I strengthened Lorraine, and made it especially vulnerable to the growing force of the black road. I saw that it would lie in your path, no matter where you went. After your escape, all roads led to Lorraine."

"Why?"

"It was a trap I had set for you, and maybe a test. I

wanted to be with you when you met the forces of Chaos. I also wanted to travel with you for a time."

"A test? What were you testing me for? And why travel with me?"

"Can you not guess? I have watched all of you over the years. I never named a successor. I purposely left the matter muddled. You are all enough like me for me to know that the moment I declared for one of you I would be signing his or her death warrant. No. I intentionally left things as they were until the very end. Now, though, I have decided. It is to be you."

"You communicated with me, as yourself, briefly, back in Lorraine. You told me then to take the throne. If you had made up your mind at that point why did you continue the masquerade?"

"But I had not decided then. That was merely a means to assure your continuing. I feared you might come to like that girl too much, and that land. When you emerged a hero from the Black Circle you might have decided to settle and stay there. I wanted to plant the notions that would cause you to continue your journey."

I was silent for a long while. We had moved a good distance about the Pattern.

Then, "There is something that I have to know," I said. "Before I came here I was speaking with Dara, who is in the process of trying to clear her name with us—"

"It *is* clear," he said. "I have cleared it."

I shook my head.

"I refrained from accusing her of something I have been thinking about for some time. There is a very good reason why I feel she cannot be trusted, despite her protests and your endorsement. Two reasons, in fact."

"I know, Corwin. But she did not kill Benedict's ser-

vants to manage her position at his house. I did it myself,
to assure her getting to you as she did, at just the appro-
priate time."

"You? You were party to her whole plot? Why?"

"She will make you a good queen, son. I trust the blood
of Chaos for strength. It was time for a fresh infusion.
You will take the throne already provided with an heir.
By the time he is ready for it, Merlin will long have been
weaned from his upbringing."

We had come all the way around to the place of the
black smear. I stopped. I squatted and studied it.

"You think this thing is going to kill you?" I finally
asked.

"I know that it is."

"You are not above murdering innocent people to manipulate me. Yet you would sacrifice your life for the
kingdom."

I looked up at him.

"My own hands are not clean," I said, "and I certainly
do not presume to judge you. A while back, though, when
I made ready to try the Pattern, I thought how my feelings had changed—toward Eric, toward the throne. You
do what you do, I believe, as a duty. I, too, feel a duty
now, toward Amber, toward the throne. More than that,
actually. Much more, I realized, just then. But I realized
something else, also, something that duty does not require
of me. I do not know when or how it stopped and I
changed, but I do not want the throne, Dad. I am sorry it
messes up your plans, but I do not want to be king of
Amber. I am sorry."

I looked away then, back down at the smear. I heard
him sigh.

Then, "I am going to send you home now," he said.

"Saddle your horse and take provisions. Ride to a place outside Amber—any place, fairly isolated."

"My tomb?"

He snorted and chuckled faintly.

"That will do. Go there and wait my pleasure. I have some thinking to do."

I stood. He reached out and placed his right hand on my shoulder. The Jewel was pulsing. He looked into my eyes.

"No man can have everything he wants the way that he wants it," he said.

And there was a distancing effect, as of the power of a Trump, only working in reverse. I heard voices, then about me I saw the room I had earlier departed. Benedict, Gérard, Random and Dara were still there. I felt Dad release my shoulder. Then he was gone and I was among them once again.

"What is the story?" Random said. "We saw Dad sending you back. By the way, how did he do that?"

"I do not know," I said. "But he confirms what Dara has told us. He gave her the signet and the message."

"Why?" Gérard asked.

"He wanted us to learn to trust her," I said.

Benedict rose to his feet. "Then I will go and do as I have been bid."

"He wants you to attack, then fall back," Dara said. "After that, it will only be necessary to contain them."

"For how long?"

"He said only that this will become apparent."

Benedict gave one of his rare smiles and nodded. He managed his card case with his one hand, removed the deck, thumbed out the special Trump I had given him for the Courts.

"Good luck," Random said.

"Yes," Gérard agreed.

I added my wishes and watched him fade. When his rainbow afterimage had vanished I looked away and noticed that Dara was crying silently. I did not remark on it.

"I, too, have orders now—of a sort," I said. "I had best be moving."

"And I will get back to the sea," said Gérard.

"No," I heard Dara say as I was moving toward the door.

I halted.

"You are to remain here, Gérard, and see to the safety of Amber herself. No attack will come by sea."

"But I thought Random was in charge of the local defense."

She shook her head.

"Random is to join Julian in Arden."

"Are you sure?" Random asked.

"I am certain."

"Good," he said. "It is nice to know he at least thought of me. Sorry, Gérard. That's the breaks."

Gérard simply looked puzzled. "I hope he knows what he is doing," he said.

"We have been through that already," I told him. "Good-bye."

I heard a footfall as I left the room. Dara was beside me.

"What now?" I asked her.

"I thought I would walk with you, wherever you are going."

"I am just going up the hill to get some supplies. Then I am heading for the stables."

"I will go with you."

"I am riding alone."

"I could not accompany you, anyway. I still have to speak with your sisters."

"They're included, huh?"

"Yes."

We walked in silence for a time, then she said, "The whole business was not so cold-blooded as it seemed, Corwin."

We entered the supply room.

"What business?"

"You know what I mean."

"Oh. That. Well, good."

"I like you. It could be more than that one day, if you feel anything."

My pride handed me a snappy reply, but I bit it back. One learns a few things over the centuries. She had used me, true, but then it seemed she had not been entirely a free agent at the time. The worst that might be said, I suppose, was that Dad wanted me to want her. But I did not let my resentment on this interfere with what my own feelings really were, or could become.

So, "I like you, too," I said, and I looked at her. She seemed as if she needed to be kissed just then, so I did. "I had better get ready now."

She smiled and squeezed my arm. Then she was gone. I decided not to examine my feelings just then. I got some things together.

I saddled Star and rode back up over the crest of Kolvir until I came to my tomb. Seated outside it, I smoked my pipe and watched the clouds. I felt I had had a very full day, and it was still early afternoon. Premonitions played tag in the grottoes of my mind, none of which I would have cared to take to lunch.

3

Contact came suddenly as I sat drowsing. I was on my feet in an instant. It was Dad.

"Corwin, I have made my decisions and the time has come," he said. "Bare your left arm."

I did this, as his form continued to grow in substantiality, looking more and more regal the while, a strange sadness on his face, of a sort I had never seen there before.

He took hold of my arm with his left hand and drew his dagger with his right.

I watched as he cut my arm, then resheathed his blade. The blood came forth, and he cupped his left hand and caught it. He released my arm, covered his left hand with his right and drew away from me. Raising his hands to his face, he blew his breath into them and drew them quickly apart.

A crested red bird the size of a raven, its feathers all the color of my blood, stood on his hand, moved to his wrist, looked at me. Even its eyes were red, and there was a look of familiarity as it cocked its head and regarded me.

"He is Corwin, the one you must follow," he told the bird. "Remember him."

Then he transferred it to his left shoulder, from whence it continued to stare at me, making no effort to depart.

"You must go now, Corwin," he said, "quickly. Mount your horse and ride south, passing into Shadow as soon as you can. Hellride. Get as far away from here as possible."

"Where am I going, Father?" I asked him.

"To the Courts of Chaos. You know the way?"

"In theory. I have never ridden the distance."

He nodded slowly.

"Then get moving," he said. "I want you to create as great a time differential as you can between this place and yourself."

"All right," I said, "but I do not understand."

"You will, when the time comes."

"But there is an easier way," I protested. "I can get there faster and with a lot less bother simply by getting in touch with Benedict with his Trump and having him take me through."

"No good," Dad said. "It will be necessary for you to take the longer route because you will be carrying something which will be conveyed to you along the way."

"Conveyed? How?"

He reached up and stroked the red bird's feathers.

"By your friend here. He could not fly all the way to the Courts—not in time, that is."

"What will he bring me?"

"The Jewel. I doubt that I will be able to effect the transfer myself when I have finished what I have to do with it. Its powers may be of some benefit to us in that place."

"I see," I said. "But I still need not ride the entire distance. I can Trump through after I receive it."

"I fear not. Once I have done what must be done here, the Trumps will all become inoperative for a period of time."

"Why?"

"Because the entire fabric of existence will be undergoing an alteration. Move now, damn it! Get on your horse and ride!"

I stood and stared a moment longer.

"Father, is there no other way?"

He simply shook his head and raised his hand. He began to fade.

"Good-bye."

I turned and mounted. There was more to say, but it was too late. I turned Star toward the trail that would take me southward.

While Dad was able to play with the stuff of Shadow atop Kolvir, I had never been able to. I required a greater distance from Amber in order to work the shifts.

Still, knowing that it could be done, I felt that I ought to try. So, working my way southward across bare stone and down rocky passes where the wind howled, I sought to warp the fabric or being about me as I headed toward the trail that led to Garnath.

. . . A small clump of blue flowers as I rounded a stony shoulder.

I grew excited at this, for they were a modest part of my working. I continued to lay my will upon the world to come beyond each twisting of my way.

A shadow from a triangular stone, across my path . . . A shifting of the wind . . .

Some of the smaller ones were indeed working. A backward twist to the trail . . . A crevice . . . An ancient bird's nest, high on a rocky shelf . . . More of the blue flowers . . .

Why not? A tree . . . Another . . .

I felt the power moving within me. I worked more changes.

A thought came to me then, concerning my newfound strength. It seemed possible that it might have been purely psychological reasons which had barred me from performing such manipulations earlier. Until very recently I had considered Amber herself the single, immutable reality from which all shadows took their form. Now I realized she was but first among shadows, and that the place where my father stood represented the higher reality. Therefore, while the proximity made it difficult it did not make it impossible to effect changes in this place. Yet, under other circumstances I would have saved my strength until I had reached a point where it was easier to shift things about.

Now, now though, the need for haste lay upon me. I would have to exert myself, to rush, to do my father's bidding.

By the time I reached the trail leading down the southern face of Kolvir, the character of the land had already changed. I looked upon a series of gentle slopes, rather than the steep descent which normally marked the way. I was already entering the shadowlands.

The black road still lay like a dark scar to my left as I headed downward, but this Garnath through which it had been cut was in slightly better shape than that which I knew so well. Its lines were softer, from flocks of greenery which lay somewhat nearer the dead swath. It was as though my curse upon the land were slightly mitigated. Illusion of feeling, of course, for this was no longer exactly my Amber. But, *I am sorry for my part in this,* I addressed everything mentally, half-prayerlike. *I ride now to try to undo it. Forgive me, oh spirit of this place.*

My eyes moved in the direction of the Grove of the Unicorn, but it was too far to the west, masked by too many trees, for me even to glimpse that sacred glade.

The slope grew more level as I descended, becoming a series of gentle foothills. I let Star move faster as we crossed them, bearing to the southwest, then finally the south. Lower, lower. At a great distance to my left the sea sparkled and shone. Soon the black road would come between us, for I was descending into Garnath in its direction. No matter what I did with Shadow, I would not be able to erase that ominous presence. In fact, the fastest course I could follow would be one that paralleled it.

We came at last to the floor of the valley. The Forest of Arden towered far to my right, sweeping westward, immense and venerable. I rode on, working what changes I could to bear me even farther from my home.

While keeping the black road on hand, I stayed a good distance from it. I had to, since it was the one thing I could not change. I kept shrubs, trees and low hills between us.

I reached out then, and the texture of the land changed.

Veins of agate . . . Heaps of schist . . . A darkening of the greenery . . .

Clouds swimming across the sky . . . The sun shimmering and dancing . . .

We increased our pace. The land sank lower still. Shadows lengthened, merged. The forest retreated. A rocky wall grew to my right, another to my left. . . . A cold wind pursued me down a rough canyon. Strata streaks—red, gold, yellow and brown—flashed by. The floor of the canyon grew sandy. Dust devils spun about us. I leaned farther forward as the way began to rise once again. The walls slanted inward, grew closer together.

The way narrowed, narrowed. I could almost touch either wall. . . .

Their tops came together. I rode through a shadowy tunnel, slowing as it darkened. . . . Phosphorescent designs burst into being. The wind made a moaning noise. Out then!

The light from the walls was blinding, and giant crystals rose all about us. We plunged past, following an upward trail that led away from this region and through a series of mossy dells where small, perfectly circular pools lay still as green glass.

Tall ferns appeared before us and we made our way among them. I heard a distant trumpeting noise.

Turning, pacing . . . Red now the ferns, wider and lower . . . Beyond, a great plain, pinking into evening . . .

Forward, over pale grasses . . . The smell of fresh earth . . . Mountains or dark clouds far ahead . . . A rush of stars from my left . . . A quick spray of moisture . . . A blue moon leaps into the sky . . . Flickerings among the dark masses . . . Memories and a rumbling noise . . . Stormsmell and rushing air . . .

A strong wind . . . Clouds across the stars . . . A bright fork spearing a shattered tree to my right, turning it to flame . . . A tingling sensation . . . The smell of ozone . . . Sheets of water upon me . . . A row of lights to my left . . .

Clattering down a cobbled street . . . A strange vehicle approaching . . . Cylindrical, chugging . . . We avoid one another . . . A shout pursues me . . . Through a lighted window the face of a child . . .

Clattering . . . Splashing . . . Storefronts and homes . . . The rain lets up, dies down, is gone . . . A fog blows by, lingers, deepens, is pearled by a growing light to my left . . .

The terrain softens, grows red . . . The light within the mist brightens . . . A new wind, from behind, a growing warmth . . . The air breaks apart . . .

Sky of pale lemon . . . Orange sun rushing toward noon . . .

A shudder! A thing not of my doing, totally unanticipated . . . The ground moves beneath us, but there is more to it than that. The new sky, the new sun, the rusty desert I have just now entered—all of them expand and contract, fade and return. There comes a cracking sound, and with each fading I find Star and myself alone, amid a white nothingness—characters without a setting. We tread upon nothing. The light comes from everywhere and illuminates only ourselves. A steady cracking noise, as of the spring thaw come upon a Russian river I had once ridden beside, fills my ears. Star, who has paced many shadows, emits a frightened sound.

I look all about me. Blurred outlines appear, sharpen, grow clear. My environment is restored, though with a somewhat washed-out look to it. A bit of the pigment has been drained from the world.

We wheel to the left, racing for a low hill, mounting it, halting finally at its summit.

The black road. It too seems denatured—but even more so than the rest. It ripples beneath my gaze, almost seems to undulate as I watch. The cracking noise continues, grows louder. . . .

A wind comes out of the north, gentle at first but in-

creasing in force. Looking in that direction, I see a mass
of dark clouds building.

I know that I must move as I have never moved before.
Ultimates of destruction and creation are occurring at the
place I visited—when? No matter. The waves move outward from Amber and this, too, may pass away—and me
along with it. If Dad cannot put it all back together
again.

I shake the reins. We race southward.

A plain . . . Trees . . . Some broken buildings . . .
Faster . . .

The smoke of a forest afire . . . A wall of flame . . .
Gone . . .

Yellow sky, blue clouds . . . An armada of dirigibles
crossing . . .

Faster . . .

The sun drops like a piece of hot iron into a bucket of
water, stars become streaks . . . A pale light upon a
straight trail . . . Sounds dopplered from dark smears, the
wailing . . . Brighter the light, fainter the prospect . . .
Gray, to my right, my left . . . Brighter now . . . Nothing
but the trail my eyes to ride . . . The wailing heightens to
a shriek . . . Forms run together . . . We race through a
tunnel of Shadow . . . It begins to revolve. . . .

Turning, turning . . . Only the road is real . . . The
worlds go by . . . I have released my control of the sets
and ride now the thrust of the power itself, aimed only to
remove me from Amber and hurl me toward Chaos . . .
There is wind upon me and the cry in my ears . . . Never
before have I pushed my power over Shadow to its limit
. . . The tunnel grows as slick and seamless as glass . . . I
feel I am riding down a vortex, a maelstrom, the heart of
a tornado . . . Star and I are drenched with sweat . . .

There is a wild feeling of flight upon me, as though I am pursued . . . The road is become an abstraction . . . My eyes sting as I try to blink away the perspiration . . . I cannot hold this ride much longer . . . There comes a throbbing at the base of my skull. . . .

I draw back gently upon the reins and Star begins to slow. . . .

The walls of my tunnel of light grow grainy . . . Blotches of gray, black, white, rather than a uniformity of shading . . . Brown . . . A hint of blue . . . Green . . . The wailing descends to a hum, a rumble, fading . . . Gentler the wind . . . Shapes come and go. . . .

Slowing, slowing . . .

There is no path. I ride on mossy earth. The sky is blue, the clouds are white. I am very light-headed. I draw rein. I—

Tiny.

I was shocked as I lowered my eyes. I stood at the outskirts of a toy village. Houses I could hold in the palm of my hand, miniscule roads, tiny vehicles crawling along them. . . .

I looked back. We had crushed a number of these diminutive residences. I looked all around. There were fewer to the left. I guided Star carefully in that direction, kept moving until we had left that place. I felt bad about it—whatever it was—whoever dwelled there. But there was not a thing that I could do.

I moved again, passing through Shadow, until I came to what seemed a deserted quarry beneath a greenish sky. I felt heavier here. I dismounted, took a drink of water, walked around a bit.

I breathed deeply of the damp air that engulfed me. I was far from Amber now, about as far as one ever need go, and well on my way to Chaos. I had seldom come this far before. While I had chosen this place for a rest stop because it represented the nearest thing to normalcy I could catch hold of, the changes would soon be getting more and more radical.

I was stretching my cramped muscles when I heard the shriek, high in the air above me.

I looked up and saw the dark form descending, Grayswandir coming by reflex into my hand. But the light caught it at a proper angle as it came down, and the winged form took fire on its way.

My familiar bird circled, circled, descended to my outstretched arm. Those frightening eyes regarded me with a peculiar intelligence, but I did not spare them the attention I might have on another occasion. Instead, I sheathed Grayswandir and reached for the thing the bird bore.

The Jewel of Judgment.

I knew by this that Dad's effort, whatever it had amounted to, was finished. The Pattern had either been repaired or botched. He was either alive or dead. Choose a couple from either column. The effects of his act would be spreading outward from Amber through Shadow now, like the ripples in the proverbial pond. I would learn more of them soon enough. In the meantime, I had my orders.

I drew the chain over my head and let the Jewel fall upon my breast. I remounted Star. My bloodbird emitted a short cry and rose into the air.

We moved again.

. . . Over a landscape where the sky whitened as the ground darkened. Then the land flared and the sky grew black. Then the reverse. And again . . . With each stride the effect shifted, and as we moved faster it built to a stroboscopic series of still-shots about us, gradually growing to a jerky animation, then the hyperactive quality of a silent film. Finally, all was a blur.

Points of light flashed past, like meteors or comets. I began to feel a throbbing sensation, as of a cosmic heartbeat. Everything began to turn about me, as though I had been caught up in a whirlwind.

Something was going wrong. I seemed to be losing control. Could it be that the effects of Dad's doings had already reached the area of Shadow through which I passed? It seemed hardly likely. Still . . .

Star stumbled. I clung tightly as we went down, not wishing to be separated in Shadow. I struck my shoulder on a hard surface and lay there for a moment, stunned.

When the world came together about me again, I sat up and looked around.

A uniform twilight prevailed, but there were no stars. Instead, large rocks of various shapes and sizes drifted and hovered in the air. I got to my feet and looked all about.

It was possible, from what I could see of it, that the irregular stony surface on which I stood was itself but a mountain-sized boulder drifting with the others. Star rose and stood shivering at my side. An absolute silence contained us. The still air was cool. There was not another living thing in sight. I did not like this place. I would not have halted here of my own volition. I knelt to inspect Star's legs. I wanted to leave as soon as possible, preferably mounted.

As I was about this, I heard a soft chuckle which might have come from a human throat.

I paused, resting my hand upon Grayswandir's hilt and seeking the source of the sound.

Nothing. Nowhere.

Yet I had heard it. I turned slowly, looking in every direction. No . . .

Then it came again. Only this time, I realized that it had its source overhead.

I scanned the floating rocks. Shadow-draped, it was difficult to distinguish—

There!

Ten meters above the ground and thirty or so to my left, what appeared to be a human form stood atop a small island in the sky, regarding me. I considered it. Whatever it was, it seemed too far off to pose a threat. I was certain that I could be gone before it could reach me. I moved to mount Star.

"No good, Corwin," called the voice I least wanted to hear just then. "You are locked here. There is no way you can depart without my leave."

I smiled as I mounted, then drew Grayswandir.

"Let's find out," I said. "Come bar my way."

"Very well," he replied, and flames sprang from the bare rock, towering full circle about me, licking, sprawling, soundless.

Star went wild. I slammed Grayswandir back into the scabbard, whipped a corner of my cloak across Star's eyes, spoke soothing words. As I did this, the circle enlarged, the fires receding toward the edges of the great rock on which we stood.

"Convinced?" came the voice. "This place is too small. Ride in any direction. Your mount will panic again before you can shift into Shadow."

"Good-bye, Brand," I said, and I began to ride.

I rode in a large counterclockwise circle about the rocky surface, shielding Star's right eye from the flames about the periphery of things. I heard Brand chuckle again, not realizing what I was doing.

A pair of large rocks . . . Good. I rode on by, continuing the course. Now a jagged hedge of stone to my left, a rise, a dip . . . A mess of shadow the fires cast, across my path . . . There. Down . . . Up. A touch of green to that patch of light . . . I could feel the shifting begin.

The fact that it is easier for us to take a straight course does not make it the only way. We all pursue it so much of the time, though, that we tend to forget that one can also make progress by going around in circles. . . .

I could feel the shift more strongly as I neared the two large rocks again. Brand caught on about then, also.

"Hold it, Corwin!"

I threw him a finger and cut between the rocks, heading down into a narrow canyon speckled with points of yellow light. According to specifications.

I drew my cloak away from Star's head and shook the reins. The canyon cut abruptly to the right. We followed it into a better-lighted avenue which widened and brightened as we went.

. . . Beneath a jutting overhang, sky of milk shading to pearl on its other side.

Riding deeper, faster, farther . . . A jagged cliff crowned the upper talus to my left, greening in twisted sign of shrubbery beneath a pink-touched sky.

I rode until the greenery was bluery beneath a yellow sky, till the canyon rose to meet a lavender plain where orange rocks rolled as the ground was shaken beneath us in time with our hoofbeats. I crossed there under wheeling comets, coming to the shore of a blood-red sea in a place of heavy perfumes. I rode a large green sun and a small bronze one out of the sky as I paced that shore, while skeletal navies clashed and serpents of the deep circled their orange and blue-sailed vessels. The Jewel pulsed upon me and I drew strength from it. A wild wind came up and lofted us through a copper-clouded sky above a wailing chasm which seemed to extend forever, black-bottomed, spark-shot, fuming with heady scents. . . .

At my back, the sound of thunder, ceaseless . . . Fine lines, like the craqueleur of an old painting, abreast of us, advancing, everywhere . . . Cold, a fragrance-killing wind pursues . . .

Lines . . . The cracks widen, blackness flows to fill . . . Dark streaks race by, up, down, back upon themselves . . . The settling of a net, the labors of a giant, invisible spider, world-trapping . . .

Down, down and down . . . The ground again, wrinkled and leathery as a mummy's neck . . . Soundless, our throbbing passage . . . Softer the thunder, falling the wind . . . Dad's last gasp? Speed now and away . . .

A narrowing of lines, to the fineness of an etching, fading then in the three suns' heat . . . And faster yet . . .

A rider, approaching . . . Hand to hilt in time to my own . . . Me. Myself coming back? Simultaneous, our salutes . . . Through one another, somehow, the air like a sheet of water that one dry instant . . . What Carroll mirror, what Rebma, Tir-na Nog'th effect . . . Yet far, far to my left, a black thing writhing . . . We pace the road . . . It leads me on . . .

White sky, white ground and no horizon . . . Sunless and cloudless the prospect . . . Only that thread of black, far off, and gleaming pyramids everywhere, massive, disconcerting . . .

We tire. I do not like this place . . . But we have outrun whatever process pursues. Draw rein.

I was tired, but I felt a strange vitality within me. It seemed as though it arose from within my breast . . . The Jewel. Of course. I made an effort to draw upon this power again. I felt it flow outward through my limbs, barely halting at my extremities. It was almost as if—

Yes. I reached out and lay my will upon my blank and geometrical surroundings. They began to alter.

It was a movement. The pyramids shuffled by, darkening as they passed. They shrank, they merged, they passed to gravel. The world turned upside down and I stood as on the underside of a cloud, watching landscapes flash by beneath/above.

Light streamed upward past me, from a golden sun beneath my feet. This, too, passed, and the fleecy ground darkened, firing waters upward to erode the passing land. Lightnings jumped up to strike the world overhead, to break it apart. In places it shattered and its pieces fell about me.

They began to swirl as a wave of darkness passed.

When the light came again, bluish this time, it held no point source and described no land.

. . . Golden bridges cross the void in great streamers, one of them flashing beneath us even now. We wind along its course, standing the while still as a statue . . . For an age, perhaps, this goes on. A phenomenon not unrelated to highway hypnosis enters through my eyes, lulls me dangerously.

I do what I can to accelerate our passage. Another age goes by.

Finally, far ahead, a dusky, misty blotch, our terminus, growing very slowly despite our velocity.

By the time we reach it, it is gigantic—an island in the void, forested over with golden, metallic trees. . . .

I stop the motion which has borne us thus far and we move forward under our own power, entering that wood. Grass like aluminum foil crunches beneath us as we pass among those trees. Strange fruit, pale and shiny, hangs about me. There are no animal sounds immediately apparent. Working our way inward, we come to a small clearing through which a quicksilver stream flows. There, I dismount.

"Brother Corwin," comes that voice again. "I have been waiting for you."

4

I faced the wood, watched him emerge from it. I did not draw my weapon, as he had not drawn his. I reached down into the Jewel with my mind, though. After the exercise I had just completed, I realized that I could do a lot more than control weather with it. Whatever Brand's power, I felt I'd a weapon now with which to confront it directly. The Jewel pulsed more deeply as I did this.

"Truce," Brand said. "Okay? May we talk?"

"I do not see that we have anything more to say to one another," I told him.

"If you do not give me a chance you will never know for certain, will you?"

He came to a halt about seven meters away, flung his green cloak back over his left shoulder and smiled.

"All right. Say it, whatever it is," I said.

"I tried to stop you," he said, "back there, for the Jewel. It is obvious that you know what it is now, that you realize how important it is."

I said nothing.

"Dad has already used it," he continued, "and I am sorry to report that he has failed in what he set out to do with it."

"What? How could you know?"

"I can see through Shadow, Corwin. I would have thought our sister had filled you in more thoroughly on these matters. With a little mental effort, I can perceive whatever I choose now. Naturally, I was concerned with the outcome of this affair. So I watched. He is dead, Corwin. The effort was too much for him. He lost control of the forces he was manipulating and was blasted by them a little over halfway through the Pattern."

"You lie!" I said, touching the Jewel.

He shook his head.

"I admit that I am not above lying to gain my ends, but this time I am telling the truth. Dad is dead. I saw him fall. The bird brought you the Jewel then, as he had willed it. We are left in a universe without a Pattern."

I did not want to believe him. But it was possible that Dad had failed. I had the assurance of the only expert in the business, Dworkin, as to the difficulty of the task.

"Granting for the moment what you have said, what happens next?" I asked.

"Things fall apart," he replied. "Even now, Chaos wells up to fill the vacuum back at Amber. A great vortex has come into being, and it grows. It spreads ever outward, destroying the shadow worlds, and it will not stop until it meets with the Courts of Chaos, bringing all of creation full circle, with Chaos once more to reign over all."

I felt dazed. Had I struggled from Greenwood, through everything, to here, to have it end this way? Would I see everything stripped of meaning, form, content, life, when things had been pushed to a kind of completion?

"No!" I said. "It cannot be so."

"Unless . . ." Brand said softly.

"Unless what?"

"Unless a new Pattern is inscribed, a new order created to preserve form."

"You mean ride back into that mess and try to complete the job? You just said that the place no longer exists."

"No. Of course not. The location is unimportant. Wherever there is a Pattern there is a center. I can do it right here."

"You think that you can succeed where Dad failed?"

"I have to try. I am the only one who knows enough about it and has sufficient time before the waves of Chaos arrive. Listen, I admit to everything Fiona has doubtless told you about me. I have schemed and I have acted. I have dealt with the enemies of Amber. I have shed our blood. I tried to burn out your memory. But the world as we know it is being destroyed now, and I live here too. All of my plans—everything!—will come to nothing if some measure of order is not preserved. Perhaps I have been duped by the Lords of Chaos. It is difficult for me to admit that, but I see the possibility now. It is not too late to foil them, though. We can build the new bastion of order right here."

"How?"

"I need the Jewel—and your assistance. This will be the site of the new Amber."

"Supposing—*arguendo*—I give it to you. Would the new Pattern be exactly like the old one?"

He shook his head.

"It could not be, any more than the one Dad was attempting to create would have been like Dworkin's. No two authors can render the same story in the same fashion. Individual stylistic differences cannot be avoided. No matter how hard I might try to duplicate it, my version would be slightly different."

"How could you do this," I asked, "when you are not fully attuned to the Jewel? You would need a Pattern to complete the process of attunement—and, as you say, the Pattern has been destroyed. What gives?"

Then, "I said that I would need your help," he stated. "There is another way to attune a person to the Jewel. It requires the assistance of someone who is already attuned. You would have to project yourself through the Jewel once more, and take me with you—into and through the primary Pattern that lies beyond."

"And then?"

"Why, when the ordeal is past I will be attuned, you give me the Jewel, I inscribe a new Pattern and we are back in business. Things hold together. Life goes on."

"What of Chaos?"

"The new Pattern will be unmarred. They will no longer have the road giving them access to Amber."

"With Dad dead, how would the new Amber be run?"

He smiled crookedly.

"I ought to have something for my pains, oughtn't I? I will be risking my life with this, and the odds are not all that good."

I smiled back at him.

"Considering the payoff, what is to prevent me from taking the gamble myself?" I said.

"The same thing that prevented Dad from succeeding —all the forces of Chaos. They are summoned by a kind of cosmic reflex when such an act is begun. I have had more experience with them than you. You would not have a chance. I might."

"Now let us say that you are lying to me, Brand. Or let us be kind and say that you did not see clearly through all the turmoil. Supposing Dad did succeed? Supposing there is a new Pattern in existence right now? What would happen if you were to do another, here, now?"

"I . . . It has never been done before. How should I know?"

"I wonder?" I said. "Might you still get your own version of reality that way? Might it represent the splitting off of a new universe—Amber and Shadow—just for you? Might it negate ours? Or would it simply stand apart? Or would there be some overlapping? What do you think, given that situation?"

He shrugged his shoulders.

"I have already answered that. It has never been done before. How should I know?"

"But I think that you do know, or can make a very good guess at it. I think that that is what you are planning, that that is what you want to try—because that is all you have left now. I take this action on your part as an indication that Dad has succeeded and that you are down to your last card. But you need me and you need the Jewel for it. You cannot have either."

He sighed.

"I had expected more of you. But all right. You are wrong, but leave it at that. Listen, though. Rather than see everything lost, I will split the realm with you."

"Brand," I said, "get lost. You cannot have the Jewel, or my help. I have heard you out, and I think that you are lying."

"You are afraid," he said, "afraid of me. I do not blame you for not wanting to trust me. But you are making a mistake. You need me now."

"Nevertheless, I have made my choice."

He took a step toward me. Another . . .

"Anything you want, Corwin. I can give you anything you care to name."

"I was with Benedict in Tir-na Nog'th," I said, "looking

through his eyes, listening with his ears, when you made him the same offer. Shove it, Brand. I am going on with my mission. If you think that you can stop me, now is as good a time as any."

I began walking toward him. I knew that I would kill him if I reached him. I also felt that I would not reach him.

He halted. He took a step backward.

"You are making a big mistake," he said.

"I do not think so. I think that I am doing exactly the right thing."

"I will not fight with you," he said hastily. "Not here, not above the abyss. You have had your chance, though. The next time that we meet, I will have to take the Jewel from you."

"What good will it be to you, unattuned?"

"There might still be a way for me to manage it—more difficult, but possible. You have had your chance. Goodbye."

He retreated into the wood. I followed after, but he had vanished.

I left that place and rode on, along a road over nothing. I did not like to consider the possibility that Brand might have been telling the truth, or at least a part of it. But the things he had said kept returning to plague me. Supposing Dad had failed? Then I was on a fool's errand. Everything was already over, and it was just a matter of time. I did not like looking back, just in case something was gaining on me. I passed into a moderately paced hellride. I wanted to get to the others before the waves of Chaos reached that far, just to let them know that I had kept faith, to let them see that in the end I had tried my best. I wondered then how the actual battle was going. Or had it even begun yet, within that time frame?

I swept along the bridge, which widened now beneath a brightening sky. As it assumed the aspect of a golden plain, I considered Brand's threat. Had he said what he had said simply to raise doubts, increase my discomfort and impair my efficiency? Possibly. Yet, if he required the Jewel he would have to ambush me. And I had a respect for that strange power he had acquired over Shadow. It seemed almost impossible to prepare for an attack by someone who could watch my every move and transport himself instantaneously to the most advantageous spot. How soon might it come? Not too soon, I guessed. First, he would want to frazzle my nerves—and I was already tired and more than a little punchy. I would have to rest, to sleep, sooner or later. It was impossible for me to go that great distance in a single stretch, no matter how accelerated the hellride.

Fogs of pink and orange and green fled past, swirled about me, filling up the world. The ground rang beneath us like metal. Occasional musical tones, as of rung crystal occurred overhead. My thoughts danced. Memories of many worlds came and went in random fashion. Ganelon, my friend-enemy, and my father, enemy-friend, merged and parted, parted and merged. Somewhere one of them asked me who had a right to the throne. I had thought it was Ganelon, wanting to know our several justifications. Now I knew that it had been Dad, wanting to know my feelings. He had judged. He had made his decision. And I was backing out. Whether it was arrested development, the desire to be free of such an encumbrance, or a matter of sudden enlightenment based on all that I had experienced in recent years, growing slowly within me, granting

me a more mature view of the onerous role of monarch
apart from its moments of glory, I do not know. I remembered my life on the shadow Earth, following orders, giving them. Faces swam before me—people I had known
over the centuries—friends, enemies, wives, lovers, relatives. Lorraine seemed to be beckoning me on, Moire
laughing, Deirdre weeping. I fought again with Eric. I
recalled my first passage through the Pattern, as a boy,
and the later one when, step by step, my memory was
given back to me. Murders, thieveries, knaveries, seduc-
tions returned because, as Mallory said, they were there. I
was unable, even, to place them all correctly in terms of
time. There was no great anxiety because there was no
great guilt. Time, time, and more time had softened the
edges of harsher things, had worked its changes on me. I
saw my earlier selves as different people, acquaintances I
had outgrown. I wondered how I could ever have been
some of them. As I rushed onward, scenes from my past
seemed to solidify in the mists about me. No poetic li-
cense here. Battles in which I had taken part assumed
tangible form, save for a total absence of sound—the flare
of weapons, the colors of uniforms, banners and blood.
And people—most of them now long dead—moved from
my memory into silent animation about me. None of these
were members of my family, but all of them were people
who had once meant something to me. Yet there was no
special pattern to it. There were noble deeds as well as
shameful; enemies as well as friends—and none of the persons involved took note of my passage; all were caught up
in some long-past sequence of actions. I wondered then at
the nature of the place through which I rode. Was it some
watered-down version of Tir-na Nog'th, with some mind-
sensitive substance in the vicinity that drew from me and

projected about me this "This Is Your Life" panorama? Or was I simply beginning to hallucinate? I was tired, anxious, troubled, distressed, and I passed along a way which provided a monotonous, gentle stimulation of the senses of the sort leading to reverie. . . . In fact, I realized that I had lost control over Shadow sometime back and was now simply proceeding in a linear fashion across this landscape, trapped in a kind of externalized narcissism by the spectacle. . . . I realized then that I had to stop and rest—probably even sleep a little—though I feared doing so in this place. I would have to break free and make my way to a more sedate, deserted spot. . . .

I wrenched at my surroundings. I twisted things about. I broke free.

Soon I was riding in a rough, mountainous area, and shortly thereafter I came to the cave that I desired.

We passed within, and I tended to Star. I ate and drank just enough to take the edge off my hunger. I built no fire. I wrapped myself in my cloak and in a blanket I had brought. I held Grayswandir in my right hand. I lay facing the darkness beyond the cavemouth.

I felt a little sick. I knew that Brand was a liar, but his words bothered me anyway.

But I had always been good at going to sleep. I closed my eyes and was gone.

5

I was awakened by a sense of presence. Or maybe it was
a noise and a sense of presence. Whatever, I was awake
and I was certain that I was not alone. I tightened my
grip on Grayswandir and opened my eyes. Beyond that, I
did not move.

A soft light, like moonlight, came in through the cavemouth. There was a figure, possibly human, standing just
inside. The lighting was such that I could not tell whether
it faced me or faced outward. But then it took a step toward me.

I was on my feet, the point of my blade toward its
breast. It halted.

"Peace," said a man's voice, in Thari. "I have but taken
refuge from the storm. May I share your cave?"

"What storm?" I asked.

As if in answer, there came a roll of thunder followed
by a gust of wind with the smell of rain within it.

"Okay, that much is true," I said. "Make yourself com-
fortable."

He sat down, well inside, his back against the right-
hand wall of the cave. I folded my blanket for a pad and
seated myself across from him. About four meters separated us. I located my pipe and filled it, then tried a
match which had been with me from the shadow Earth.
It lit, saving me a lot of trouble. The tobacco had a good

smell, mixed with the damp breeze. I listened to the sounds of the rain and regarded the dark outline of my nameless companion. I thought over some possible dangers, but it had not been Brand's voice which had addressed me.

"This is no natural storm," the other said.

"Oh? How so?"

"For one thing, it is coming out of the north. They never come out of the north, here, this time of year."

"That's how records are made."

"For another, I have never seen a storm behave this way. I have been watching it advance all day—just a steady line, moving slowly, front like a sheet of glass. So much lightning, it looks like a monstrous insect with hundreds of shiny legs. Most unnatural. And behind it, things have grown very distorted."

"That happens in the rain."

"Not that way. Everything seems to be changing its shape. Flowing. As if it is melting the world—or stamping away its forms."

I shuddered. I had thought that I was far enough ahead of the dark waves that I could take a little rest. Still, he might be wrong, and it could just be an unusual storm. But I did not want to take the chance. I rose and turned to the rear of the cave. I whistled.

No response. I went back and groped around.

"Something the matter?"

"My horse is gone."

"Could it have wandered off?"

"Must have. I'd have thought Star'd have better sense, though."

I went to the cavemouth but could see nothing. I was

half-drenched in the instant I was there. I returned to my position beside the left wall.

"It seems like an ordinary enough storm to me," I said. "They sometimes get pretty bad in the mountains."

"Perhaps you know this country better than I do?"

"No, I am just traveling through—a thing I had better be continuing soon, too."

I touched the Jewel. I reached into it, then through it, out and up, with my mind. I felt the storm about me and ordered it away, with red pulses of energy corresponding to my heartbeats. Then I leaned back, found another match and relit my pipe. It would still take a while for the forces I had manipulated to do their work, against a stormfront of this size.

"It will not last too long," I said.

"How can you tell?"

"Privileged information."

He chuckled.

"According to some versions, this is the way that the world ends—beginning with a strange storm from out of the north."

"That's right," I said, "and this is it. Nothing to worry about, though. It will be all over, one way or the other, before too long."

"That stone you are wearing . . . It is giving off light."

"Yes."

"You were joking about this being the end, though—were you not?"

"No."

"You make me think of that line from the Holy Book—*The Archangel Corwin shall pass before the storm, lightning upon his breast.* . . . You would not be named Corwin, would you?"

"How does the rest of it go?"

"*. . . When asked where he travels, he shall say, 'To the ends of the Earth,' where he goes not knowing what enemy will aid him against another enemy, nor whom the Horn will touch.*"

"That's all?"

"All there is about the Archangel Corwin."

"I have run into this difficulty with Scripture in the past. It tells you enough to get interested, but never enough to be of any immediate use. It is as though the author gets his kicks by tantalizing. One enemy against another? The Horn? Beats me."

"Where *do* you travel?"

"Not too far, unless I can find my horse."

I returned to the cavemouth. It was letting up now, with a glow like a moon behind some clouds to the west, another to the east. I looked both ways along the trail and down the slope to the valley. No horses anywhere in sight. I turned back to the cave. Just as I did, however, I heard Star's whinny far below me.

I called back to the stranger in the cave, "I have to go. You can have the blanket."

I do not know whether he replied, for I moved off into the drizzle then, picking my way down the slope. Again, I exerted myself through the Jewel, and the drizzle halted, to be replaced by a mist.

The rocks were slippery, but I made it halfway down without stumbling. I paused then, both to catch my breath and to get my bearings. From that point, I was not certain as to the exact direction from which Star's whinny had come. The moon's light was a little stronger, visibility a bit better, but I saw nothing as I studied the prospect before me. I listened for several minutes.

Then I heard the whinny once more—from below, to my left, near a dark boulder, cairn or rocky outcrop. There did seem to be some sort of turmoil in the shadows at its base. Moving as quickly as I dared, I laid my course in that direction.

As I reached level ground and hurried toward the place of the action, I passed pockets of ground mist, stirred slightly by a breeze from out of the west, snaking silvery, about my ankles. I heard a grating, crunching sound, as of something heavy being pushed or rolled over a rocky surface. Then I caught sight of a gleam of light, low on the dark mass I was approaching.

Drawing nearer, I saw small, manlike forms outlined in a rectangle of light, struggling to move a great rocky slab. Faint echoes of a clattering sound and another whinny came from their direction. Then the stone began to move, swinging like the door that it probably was. The lighted area diminished, narrowed to a sliver, vanished with a booming sound, all of the struggling figures having first passed within.

When I finally reached that rocky mass all was silent once again. I pressed my ear to the stone, but heard nothing. But, whoever they were, they had taken my horse. I had never liked horse thieves, and I had killed my share in the past. And right now, I needed Star as I had seldom needed a horse. So I groped about, seeking the edges of that stony gate.

It was not too difficult to describe its outlines with my fingertips. I probably located it sooner than I would have by daylight, when everything would have blended and merged more readily to baffle the eye. Knowing its situation, I sought further then after some handhold by which

I might draw it. They had seemed to be little guys, so I looked low.

I finally discovered what might have been the proper place and seized hold of it. I pulled then, but it was stubborn. Either they were disproportionately strong or there was a trick to it that I was missing.

No matter. There is a time for subtlety and a time for brute force. I was both angry and in a hurry, so the decision was made.

I began to draw upon the slab once again, tightening the muscles in my arms, my shoulders, my back, wishing Gérard were nearby. The door creaked. I kept pulling. It moved slightly—an inch, perhaps—and stuck. I did not slacken, but increased my effort. It creaked again.

I leaned backward, shifted my weight and braced my left foot against the rocky wall at the side of the portal. I pushed with it as I drew back. There was more creaking and some grinding as it moved again—another inch or so. Then it stopped and I could not budge it.

I released my grip and stood, flexing my arms. Then I put my shoulder to it and pushed the door back to its fully closed position. I took a deep breath and seized it again.

I put my left foot back where it had been. No gradual pressure this time. I yanked and shoved simultaneously.

There was a snapping sound and a clattering from within, and the door came forward about half a foot, grinding as it moved. It seemed freer now, though, so I got to my feet, reversed my position—back to wall—and found sufficient purchase to push it outward.

It moved more easily this time, but I could not resist placing my foot against it as it began to swing and thrusting forward as hard as I could. It shot through a full hundred and eighty degrees, slammed back against the rock on the other side with a great booming noise, fractured in several places, swayed, fell and struck the ground with a crash that made it shudder, breaking off more fragments when it hit.

Grayswandir was back in my hand before it struck, and I had dropped into a crouch and stolen a quick look about the corner.

Light . . . There was illumination beyond . . . From little lamps depending from hooks along the wall . . . Beside the stairway . . . Going down . . . To a place of greater light and some sounds . . . Like music . . .

There was no one in sight. I would have thought that the godawful din I had raised would have caught someone's attention, but the music continued. Either the sound —somehow—had not carried, or they did not give a damn. Either way . . .

I rose and stepped over the threshold. My foot struck against a metal object. I picked it up and examined it. A twisted bolt. They had barred the door after themselves. I tossed it back over my shoulder and started down the stair.

The music—fiddles and pipes—grew louder as I advanced. From the breaking of the light, I could see that there was some sort of hall off to my right, from the foot of the stair. They were small steps and there were a lot of them. I did not bother with stealth, but hurried down to the landing.

When I turned and looked into the hall, I beheld a scene out of some drunken Irishman's dream. In a smoky, torchlit hall, hordes of meter-high people, red-faced and green clad, were dancing to the music or quaffing what appeared to be mugs of ale while stamping their feet, slapping tabletops and each other, grinning, laughing and shouting. Huge kegs lined one wall, and a number of the revelers were queued up before the one which had been tapped. An enormous fire blazed in a pit at the far end of the room, its smoke being sucked back through a crevice in the rock wall, above a pair of cavemouths running anywhere. Star was tethered to a ring in the wall beside that pit, and a husky little man in a leather apron was grinding and honing some suspicious-looking instruments.

Several faces turned in my direction, there were shouts and suddenly the music stopped. The silence was almost complete.

I raised my blade to an overhand, épée en garde position, pointed across the room toward Star. All faces were turned in my direction by then.

"I have come for my horse," I said. "Either you bring him to me or I come and get him. There will be a lot more blood the second way."

From off to my right, one of the men, larger and grayer than most of the others, cleared his throat.

"Begging your pardon," he began, "but how did you get in here?"

"You will be needing a new door," I said. "Go and look if you care to, if it makes any difference—and it may. I will wait."

I stepped aside and put the wall to my back.

He nodded.

"I will do that."

And he darted by.

I could feel my anger-born strength flowing into and back out of the Jewel. One part of me wanted to cut and slash and stab my way across the room, another wanted a more humane settlement with people so much smaller than myself; and a third and perhaps wiser part suggested that the little guys might not be such pushovers. So I waited to see how my door-opening feat impressed their spokesman.

Moments later, he returned, giving me wide berth.

"Bring the man his horse," he said.

A sudden flurry of conversation occurred within the hall. I lowered my blade.

"My apologies," said the one who had given the order. "We desire no trouble with the like of you. We will be foraging elsewhere. No hard feelings, I hope?"

The man in the leather apron had untethered Star and started in my direction. The revelers drew back to make way as he led my mount through the hall.

I sighed.

"I will just call it a day and forgive and forget," I said.

The little man seized a flagon from a nearby table and passed it to me. Seeing my expression, he sipped from it himself.

"Join us in a drink, then?"

"Why not?" I said, and I took it and quaffed it as he did the same with the second one.

He gave a gentle belch and grinned.

"'Tis a mighty small draught for a man of your size," he said then. "Let me fetch you another, for the trail."

It was a pleasant ale, and I was thirsty after my efforts.

"All right," I said.

He called for more as Star was delivered to me.

"You can wrap the reins around this hook here," he said, indicating a low projection near the doorway, "and he will be safe out of the way."

I nodded and did that as the butcher withdrew. No one was staring at me any longer. A pitcher of the brew arrived and the little man refilled our flagons from it. One of the fiddlers struck up a fresh tune. Moments later, another joined him.

"Sit a spell," said my host, pushing a bench in my direction with his foot. "Keep your back to the wall as you would. There will be no funny business."

I did, and he rounded the table and seated himself across from me, the pitcher between us. It was good to sit for a few moments, to take my mind from my journey for just a little while, to drink the dark ale and listen to a lively tune.

"I will not be apologizing again," said my companion, "nor explaining either. We both know it was no misunderstanding. But you have got the right on your side, it is plain to see." He grinned and winked. "So I am for calling it a day, too. We will not starve. We will just not feast tonight. 'Tis a lovely jewel you are wearing. Tell me about it?"

"Just a stone," I said.

The dancing resumed. The voices grew louder. I finished my drink and he refilled the flagon. The fire undulated. The night's cold went out of my bones.

"Cozy place you've got here," I said.

"Oh, that it is. Served us for time out of mind, it has. Would you be liking the grand tour?"

"Thank you, no."

"I did not think so, but 'twas my hostly duty to offer. You are welcome to join in the dancing, too, if you wish."

I shook my head and laughed. The thought of my cavorting in this place brought me images out of Swift.

"Thanks anyway."

He produced a clay pipe and proceeded to fill it. I cleaned my own and did the same. Somehow all danger seemed past. He was a genial enough little fellow, and the others seemed harmless now with their music and their stepping.

Yet . . . I knew the stories from another place, far, so far from here . . . To awaken in the morning, naked, in some field, all traces of this spot vanished . . . I knew, yet . . .

A few drinks seemed small peril. They were warming me now, and the keening of the pipes and the wailings of the fiddles were pleasant after the brain-numbing twist-ings of the hellride. I leaned back and puffed smoke. I watched the dancers.

The little man was talking, talking. Everyone else was ignoring me. Good. I was hearing some fantastic yarn of knights and wars and treasures. Though I gave it less than half an ear, it lulled me, even drew a few chuckles.

Inside, though, my nastier, wiser self was warning me: All right, Corwin, you have had enough. Time to take your leave . . .

But, magically it seemed, my glass had been refilled, and I took it and sipped from it. One more, one more is all right.

No, said my other self, he is laying a spell on you. Can't you feel it?

I did not feel that any dwarf could drink me under the table. But I was tired, and I had not eaten much. Perhaps it would be prudent . . .

I felt myself nodding. I placed my pipe on the table. Each time that I blinked it seemed to take longer to reopen my eyes. I was pleasantly warm now, with just the least bit of delicious numbness in my tired muscles.

I caught myself nodding, twice. I tried to think of my mission, of my personal safety, of Star. . . . I mumbled something, still vaguely awake behind closed eyelids. It would be so good, just to remain this way for half a minute more. . . .

The little man's voice, musical, grew monotonous, dropped to a drone. It did not really matter what he was say—

Star whinnied.

I sat bolt upright, eyes wide, and the tableau before me swept all sleep from my mind.

The musicians continued their performance, but now no one was dancing. All of the revelers were advancing quietly upon me. Each held something in his hand—a flask, a cudgel, a blade. The one in the leather apron brandished his cleaver. My companion had just fetched a stout stick from where it had leaned against the wall. Several of them lofted small pieces of furniture. More of them had emerged from the caves near the fire pit, and they bore stones and clubs. All traces of gaiety had vanished, and their faces were now either expressionless, twisted into grimaces of hate or smiling very nasty smiles.

My anger returned, but it was not the white-heat thing I had felt earlier. Looking at the horde before me, I had no wish to tackle it. Prudence had come to temper my feelings. I had a mission. I should not risk my neck here if I could think of another way of handling things. But I was certain that I could not talk my way out of this one.

I took a deep breath. I saw that they were getting ready to rush me, and I thought suddenly of Brand and Benedict in Tir-na Nog'th, Brand not even fully attuned to the Jewel. I drew strength from that fiery stone once again, growing alert and ready to lay about me if it came to that. But first, I would have a go at their nervous systems.

I was not certain how Brand had managed it, so I simply reached out through the Jewel as I did when influencing the weather. Strangely, the music was still playing, as though this action of the little people was but some grisly continuation of their dance.

"Stand still." I said it aloud and I willed it, rising to my feet. "Freeze. Turn to statues. All of you."

I felt a heavy throbbing within/upon my breast. I felt the red forces move outward, exactly as on those other occasions when I had employed the Jewel.

My diminutive assailants were poised. The nearest ones stood stock-still, but there were still some movements among those to the rear. Then the pipes let out a crazy squeal and the fiddles fell silent. Still, I did not know whether I had reached them or whether they had halted of their own accord on seeing me stand.

Then I felt the great waves of force which flowed out from me, embedding the entire assembly in a tightening matrix. I felt them all trapped within this expression of my will, and I reached out and untethered Star.

Holding them with a concentration as pure as anything I used when passing through Shadow, I led Star to the doorway. I turned then for a final look at the frozen assembly and pushed Star on ahead of me up the stair. As I followed, I listened, but there were no sounds of renewed activity from below.

When we emerged, dawn was already paling the east. Strangely, as I mounted, I heard the distant sounds of fiddles. Moments later, the pipes came in on the tune. It seemed as though it mattered not at all whether they succeeded or failed in their designs against me; the party was going to go on.

As I headed us south, a small figure hailed me from the

doorway I had so recently quitted. It was their leader with whom I had been drinking. I drew rein, to better catch his words.

"And where do you travel?" he called after me.

Why not?

"To the ends of the Earth!" I shouted back.

He broke into a jig atop his shattered door.

"Fare thee well, Corwin!" he cried.

I waved to him. Why not, indeed? Sometimes it's damned hard to tell the dancer from the dance.

6

I rode fewer than a thousand meters to what had been the south, and everything stopped—ground, sky, mountains. I faced a sheet of white light. I thought then of the stranger in the cave and his words. He had felt that the world was being blotted out by that storm, that it corresponded to something out of a local apocalyptic legend. Perhaps it had. Perhaps it had been the wave of Chaos of which Brand had spoken, moving this way, passing over, destroying, disrupting. But this end of the valley was untouched. Why should it remain?

Then I recalled my actions on rushing out into the storm. I had used the Jewel, the power of the Pattern within it, to halt the storm over this area. And if it had been more than an ordinary storm? The Pattern had prevailed over Chaos before. Could this valley where I had stopped the rainfall be but a small island in a sea of Chaos now? If so, how was I to continue?

I looked to the east, from whence the day brightened. No sun stood new-risen in the heavens, but rather a great, blindingly burnished crown, a gleaming sword hanging through it. From somewhere I heard a bird singing, notes almost like laughter. I leaned forward and covered my face with my hands. Madness . . .

No! I had been in weird shadows before. The farther one traveled, the stranger they sometimes grew. Until

. . . What was it I'd thought that night in Tir-na Nog'th? Two lines from a story of Isak Dinesen's returned to me, lines which had troubled me sufficiently to cause me to memorize them, despite the fact that I had been Carl Corey at the time: ". . . Few people can say of themselves that they are free of the belief that this world which they see around them is in reality the work of their own imagination. Are we pleased with it, proud of it, then?" A summation of the family's favorite philosophical pastime. Do we make the Shadow worlds? Or are they there, independent of us, awaiting our footfalls? Or is there an unfairly excluded middle? Is it a matter of more or less, rather than either-or? A dry chuckle arose suddenly as I realized that I might never know the answer for certain. Yet, as I had thought that night, there is a place, a place where there comes an end to Self, a place where solipsism is no longer the plausible answer to the locales we visit, the things that we find. The existence of this place, these things, says that here, at least, there is a difference, and if here, perhaps it runs back through our shadows, too, informing them with the not-self, moving our egos back to a smaller stage. For this, I felt, was such a place, a place where the "Are we pleased with it, proud of it, then?" need not apply, as the rent vale of Garnath and my curse might have nearer home. Whatever I ultimately believed, I felt that I was about to enter the land of the completely not-I. My powers over Shadow might well be canceled beyond this point.

I sat up straight and squinted against the glare. I spoke a word to Star and shook the reins. We moved ahead.

For a moment, it was like riding into a fog. Only it was enormously brighter, and there was absolutely no sound. Then we were falling.

Falling, or drifting. After the initial shock, it was difficult to say. At first, there was a feeling of descent—perhaps intensified by the fact that Star panicked when it began. But there was nothing to kick against, and after a time Star ceased all movement save for shivering and heavy breathing.

I held the reins with my right hand and clutched the Jewel with my left. I do not know what I willed or how I reached with it, exactly, but that I wanted passage through this place of bright nothingness, to find my way once more and move on to the journey's end.

I lost track of time. The feeling of descent had vanished. Was I moving, or merely hovering? No way to say. Was the brightness really brightness, still? And that deadly silence . . . I shuddered. Here was even greater sensory deprivation than in the days of my blindness, in my old cell. Here was nothing—not the sound of a scuttling rat nor the grinding of my spoon against the door; no dampness, no chill, no textures. I continued to reach . . .

Flicker.

It seemed there had been some momentary breaking of the visual field to my right, near subliminal in its brevity. I reached out and felt nothing.

It had been so brief a thing that I was uncertain whether it had really occurred. It could easily have been an hallucination.

But it seemed to happen again, this time to my left. How long the interval between, I could not say.

Then I heard something like a groan, directionless. This, too, was very brief.

Next—and for the first time, I was certain—there came a gray and white landscape like the surface of the moon.

There and gone, perhaps a second's worth, in a small area of my visual field, off to my left. Star snorted.

To my right appeared a forest—gray and white—tumbling, as though we passed one another at some impossible angle. A small-screen fragment, less than two seconds' worth.

Then pieces of a burning building beneath me . . . Colorless . . .

Snatches of wailing, from overhead . . .

A ghostly mountain, a torchlit procession ascending a switchback trail up its nearest face . . .

A woman hanging from a tree limb, taut rope about her neck, head twisted to the side, hands tied behind her back . . .

Mountains, upside down, white; black clouds beneath . . .

Click. A tiny thrill of vibration, as if we had momentarily touched something solid—Star's hoof on stone, perhaps. Then gone . . .

Flicker.

Heads, rolling, dripping black gore . . . A chuckle from nowhere . . . A man nailed to a wall, upside down . . .

The white light again, rolling and heaving, wavelike . . .

Click. Flicker.

For one pulsebeat, we trod a trail beneath a stippled sky. The moment it was gone, I reached for it again, through the Jewel.

Click. Flicker. Click. Rumble.

A rocky trail, approaching a high mountain pass . . . Still monochrome, the world . . . At my back, a crashing like thunder . . .

I twisted the Jewel like a focus knob as the world

began to fade. It came back again. . . . Two, three, four
. . . I counted hoofbeats, heartbeats against the growling
background. . . . Seven, eight, nine . . . The world grew
brighter. I took a deep breath and sighed heavily. The air
was cold.

Between the thunder and its echoes, I heard the sound
of rain. None fell upon me, though.

I glanced back.

A great wall of rain stood perhaps a hundred meters to
the rear. I could distinguish only the dimmest of mountain outlines through it. I clucked to Star and we moved a
little faster, climbing to an almost level stretch that led
between a pair of peaks like turrets. The world ahead was
still a study in black and white and gray, the sky before
me divided by alternate bands of darkness and light. We
entered the pass.

I began to tremble. I wanted to draw rein, to rest, eat,
smoke, dismount and walk around. Yet, I was still too
close to that stormscreen to so indulge myself.

Star's hoofbeats echoed within the pass, where rock
walls rose sheer on either hand beneath that zebra sky. I
hoped these mountains would break this stormfront,
though I felt that they could not. This was no ordinary
storm, and I had a sick feeling that it stretched all the
way back to Amber, and that I would have been trapped
and lost forever within it but for the Jewel.

As I watched that strange sky, a blizzard of pale
flowers began to fall about me, brightening my way. A
pleasant odor filled the air. The thunder at my back softened. The rocks at my sides were shot with silver streaks.
The world was possessed of a twilight feeling to match
the illumination, and as I emerged from the pass, I saw
down into a valley of quirked perspective, distances im-

possible to gauge, filled with natural-seeming spires and minarets reflecting the moon-like light of the sky-streaks, reminiscent of a night in Tir-na Nog'th, interspersed with silvery trees, spotted with mirror-like pools, traversed by drifting wraiths, almost terraced-seeming in places, natural and rolling in others, cut by what appeared to be an extension of the line of trail I followed, rising and falling, hung over by an elegiac quality, sparked with inexplicable points of glitter and shine, devoid of any signs of habitation.

I did not hesitate, but began my descent. The ground about me here was chalky and pale as bone—and was that the faintest line of a black road far off to my left? I could just about make it out.

I did not hurry now, as I could see that Star was tiring. If the storm did not come on too quickly, I felt that we might take a rest beside one of the pools in the valley below. I was tired and hungry myself.

I kept a lookout on the way down, but saw no people, no animals. The wind made a soft, sighing noise. White flowers stirred on vines beside the trail when I reached the lower levels where regular foliage began. Looking back, I saw that the stormfront still had not passed the mountain crest, though the clouds continued to pile behind it.

I made my way on down into that strange place. The flowers had long before ceased to fall about me, but a delicate perfume hung in the air. There were no sounds other than our own and that of the constant breeze from my right. Oddly shaped rock formations stood all about me, seeming almost sculpted in their purity of line. The mists still drifted. The pale grasses sparkled damply.

As I followed the trail toward the valley's wooded center, the perspectives continued to shift about me, skewing distances, bending prospects. In fact, I turned off the trail to the left to approach what appeared to be a nearby lake and it seemed to recede as I advanced. When I finally came upon it, however, dismounted and dipped a finger to taste, the water was icy but sweet.

Tired, I sprawled after drinking my fill, to watch Star graze while I began a cold meal from my bag. The storm was still fighting to cross the mountains. I looked for a long while, wondering about it. If Dad had failed, then those were the growls of Armageddon and this whole trip was meaningless. It did me no good to think that way, for I knew that I had to go on, whatever. But I could not help it. I might arrive at my destination, I might see the battle won, and then see it all swept away. Pointless . . . No. Not pointless. I would have tried, and I would keep on trying to the end. That was enough, even if everything was lost. Damn Brand, anyway! For starting—

A footfall.

I was into a crouch and I was turned in that direction with my hand on my blade in an instant.

It was a woman that I faced, small, clad in white. She had long, dark hair and wild, dark eyes, and she was smiling. She carried a wicker basket, which she placed on the ground between us.

"You must be hungry, Knight at arms," she said in strangely accented Thari. "I saw you come. I brought you this."

I smiled and assumed a more normal stance.

"Thank you," I said. "I am. I am called Corwin. Yourself?"

"Lady," she said.

I quirked an eyebrow. "Thank you—Lady. You make your home in this place?"

She nodded and knelt to uncover the basket.

"Yes, my pavilion is farther back, along the lake." She gestured with her head, eastward—in the direction of the black road.

"I see," I said.

The food and the wine in the basket looked real, fresh, appetizing, better than my traveler's fare. Suspicion was with me, of course. "You will share it with me?" I asked.

"If you wish."

"I wish."

"Very well."

She spread a cloth, seated herself across from me, removed the food from the basket and arranged it between us. She served it then, and quickly sampled each item herself. I felt a trifle ignoble at this, but only a trifle. It was a peculiar location for a woman to be residing, apparently alone, just waiting around to succor the first stranger who happened along. Dara had fed me on our first meeting, also; and as I might be nearing the end of my journey, I was closer to the enemy's places of power. The black road was too near at hand, and I caught Lady eying the Jewel on several occasions.

But it was an enjoyable time, and we grew more familiar as we dined. She was an ideal audience, laughing at all my jokes, making me talk about myself. She maintained eye contact much of the time, and somehow our fingers met whenever anything was passed. If I were being taken in in some way, she was being very pleasant about it.

As we had dined and talked, I had also kept an eye on the progress of that inexorable-seeming stormfront. It had finally breasted the mountain crest and crossed over. It had begun its slow descent of the high slope. As she cleared the cloth, Lady saw the direction of my gaze and nodded.

"Yes, it is coming," she said, placing the last of the utensils in the basket and seating herself beside me, bringing the bottle and our cups. "Shall we drink to it?"

"I will drink with you, but not to that."

She poured.

"It does not matter," she said. "Not now," and she placed her hand on my arm and passed me my cup.

I held it and looked down at her. She smiled. She touched the rim of my cup with her own. We drank.

"Come to my pavilion now," she said, taking my hand, "where we will wile pleasurably the hours that remain."

"Thanks," I said. "Another time and that wiling would have been a fine dessert to a grand meal. Unfortunately, I must be on my way. Duty nags, time rushes, I've a mission."

"All right," she said. "It is not that important. And I know all about your mission. It is not all that important either, now."

"Oh? I must confess that I fully expected you to invite me to a private party which would result in me alone and palely loitering on the cold side of some hill sometime hence if I were to accept."

She laughed.

"And I must confess that it was my intention to so use you, Corwin. No longer, though."

"Why not?"

She gestured toward the advancing line of disruption.

"There is no need to delay you now. I see by this that

the Courts have won. There is nothing anyone can do to halt the advance of the Chaos."

I shuddered briefly and she refilled our cups.

"But I would rather you did not leave me at this time," she went on. "It will reach us here in a matter of hours. What better way to spend this final time than in one another's company? There is no need even to go as far as my pavilion."

I bowed my head, and she drew up close against me. What the hell. A woman and a bottle—that was how I had always said I wanted to end my days. I took a sip of the wine. She was probably right. Yet, I thought of the woman-thing which had trapped me on the black road as I was leaving Avalon. I had gone at first to aid her, succumbed quickly to her unnatural charms—then, when her mask was removed, saw that there was nothing at all behind it. Damned frightening, at the time. But, not to get too philosophical, everybody has a whole rack of masks for different occasions. I have heard pop psychologists inveigh against them for years. Still, I have met people who impressed me favorably at first, people whom I came to hate when I learned what they were like underneath. And sometimes they were like that woman-thing— with nothing much really there. I have found that the mask is often far more acceptable than its alternative. So . . . This girl I held to me might really be a monster inside. Probably was. Aren't most of us? I could think of worse ways to go if I wanted to give up at this point. I liked her.

I finished my wine. She moved to pour me more and I stayed her hand.

She looked up at me. I smiled.

"You almost persuaded me," I said.

Then I closed her eyes with kisses four, so as not to break the charm, and I went and mounted Star. The sedge was not withered, but he was right about the no birds. Hell of a way to run a railroad, though.

"Good-bye, Lady."

I headed south as the storm boiled its way down into the valley. There were more mountains before me, and the trail led toward them. The sky was still streaked, black and white, and these lines seemed to move about a bit; the over-all effect was still that of twilight, though no stars shone within the black areas. Still the breeze, still the perfume about me—and the silence, and the twisted monoliths and the silvery foliage, still dew-damp and glistening. Rag ends of mist blew before me. I tried to work with the stuff of Shadow, but it was difficult and I was tired. Nothing happened. I drew strength from the Jewel, trying to transmit some of it to Star, also. We moved at a steady pace until finally the land tilted upward before us, and we were climbing toward another pass, a more jagged thing than the one by which we had entered. I halted to look back, and perhaps a third of the valley now lay behind the shimmering screen of that advancing storm-thing. I wondered about Lady and her lake, her pavilion. I shook my head and continued.

The way steepened as we neared the pass, and we were slowed. Overhead, the white rivers in the sky took on a reddish cast which deepened as we rode. By the time I reached the entrance, the whole world seemed tinged with blood. Passing within that wide, rocky avenue, I was struck by a heavy wind. Pushing on against it, the ground grew more level beneath us, though we continued to climb and I still could not see beyond the pass.

As I rode, something rattled in the rocks to my left. I glanced that way, but saw nothing. I dismissed it as a falling stone. Half a minute later, Star jerked beneath me, let out a terrible neigh, turned sharply to the right, then began to topple, leftward.

I leaped clear, and as we both fell I saw that an arrow protruded from behind Star's right shoulder, low. I hit the ground rolling, and when I halted I looked up in the direction from which it must have come.

A figure with a crossbow stood atop the ridge to my right, about ten meters above me. He was already cranking the weapon back to prepare for another shot.

I knew that I could not reach him in time to stop him. So I cast about for a stone the size of a baseball, found one at the foot of the escarpment to my rear, hefted it and tried not to let my rage interfere with the accuracy of my throw. It did not, but it may have contributed some extra force.

The blow caught him on the left arm, and he let out a cry, dropping the crossbow. The weapon clattered down the rocks and landed on the other side of the trail, almost directly across from me.

"You son of a bitch!" I cried. "You killed my horse! I'm going to have your head for it!"

As I crossed the trail, I looked for the fastest way up to him and saw it off to my left. I hurried to it and commenced climbing. An instant later, the light and the angle were proper and I had a better view of the man, bent nearly double, massaging his arm. It was Brand, his hair even redder in the sanguine light.

"This is it, Brand," I said. "I only wish someone had done it a long time ago."

He straightened and watched me climb for a moment.

He did not reach for his blade. Just as I got to the top, perhaps seven meters away from him, he crossed his arms on his breast and lowered his head.

I drew Grayswandir and advanced. I admit that I was prepared to kill him in that or any other position. The red light had deepened until we seemed bathed in blood. The wind howled about us, and from the valley below came a rumble of thunder.

He simply faded before me. His outline grew less distinct, and by the time I reached the place where he had been standing he had vanished entirely.

I stood for a moment, cursing, remembering the story that he had somehow been transformed into a living Trump, capable of transporting himself anywhere in a very brief time.

I heard a noise from below. . . .

I rushed to the edge and looked down. Star was still kicking and blowing blood, and it tore my heart to see it. But that was not the only distressing sight.

Brand was below. He had picked up the crossbow and begun preparing it once more.

I looked about for another stone, but there was nothing at hand. Then I spotted one farther back, in the direction from which I had come. I hurried to it, resheathed my blade and raised the thing. It was about the size of a watermelon. I returned with it to the edge and sought Brand.

He was nowhere in sight.

Suddenly, I felt very exposed. He could have transported himself to any vantage and be sighting in on me at that instant. I dropped to the ground, falling across my rock. A moment later, I heard the bolt strike to my right. The sound was followed by Brand's chuckle.

I stood again, knowing it would take him at least a little while to recock his weapon. Looking in the direction of the laughter, I saw him, atop the ledge across the pass from me—about five meters higher than I was, and about twenty meters distant.

"Sorry about the horse," he said. "I was aiming for you. But those damned winds . . ."

By then I had spotted a niche and I made for it, taking the rock with me for a shield. From that wedge-shaped fissure, I watched him fit the bolt.

"A difficult shot," he called out, raising the weapon, "a challenge to my marksmanship. But certainly worth the effort. I've plenty more quarrels."

He chuckled, sighted and fired.

I bent low, holding the rock before my middle, but the bolt struck about two feet to my right.

"I had sort of guessed that might happen," he said, beginning to prepare his weapon once again. "Had to learn the windage, though."

I looked about for smaller stones to use for ammunition as I had earlier. There were none nearby. I wondered about the Jewel then. It was supposed to act to save me in the presence of immediate peril. But I had a funny feeling that this involved close proximity, and that Brand was aware of this and was taking advantage of the phenomenon. Still, mightn't there be something else I could do with the Jewel to thwart him? He seemed too far away for the paralysis trick, but I had beaten him once before by controlling the weather. I wondered how far off the storm was. I reached for it. I saw that it would take minutes I did not possess in order to set up the conditions necessary to draw lightning upon him. But the winds were another matter. I reached out for them, felt them. . . .

Brand was almost ready to shoot again. The wind began to scream through the pass.

I do not know where his next shot landed. Nowhere near me, though. He fell to readying his weapon again. I began setting up the factors for a lightningstroke. . . .

When he was ready, when he raised the weapon this time, I raised the winds once more. I saw him sight, I saw him draw a breath and hold it. Then he lowered the bow and stared at me.

"It just occurred to me," he called out, "you've got that wind in your pocket, haven't you? That is cheating, Corwin." He looked all about. "I should be able to find a footing where it will not matter, though. Aha!"

I kept working to set things up to blast him, but conditions were not ready yet. I looked up at that red- and black-streaked sky, something cloud-like forming above us. Soon, but not yet . . .

Brand faded and vanished again. Wildly, I sought him everywhere.

Then he faced me. He had come over to my side of the pass. He stood about ten meters to the south of me, with the wind at his back. I knew that I could not shift it in time. I wondered about throwing my rock. He would probably duck and I would be throwing away my shield. On the other hand . . .

He raised the weapon to his shoulder.

Stall! cried my own voice within my mind, while I continued to tamper with the heavens.

"Before you shoot, Brand, tell me one thing. All right?"

He hesitated, then lowered the weapon a few inches. "What?"

"Were you telling me the truth about what happened— with Dad, the Pattern, the coming of Chaos?"

He threw back his head and laughed, a series of short barks.

"Corwin," he stated then, "it pleases me more than I can say to see you die not knowing something that means that much to you."

He laughed again and began to raise the weapon. I had just moved to hurl my rock and rush him. But neither of us completed either action.

There came a great shriek from overhead, and a piece of the sky seemed to detach itself and fall upon Brand's head. He screamed and dropped the crossbow. He raised his hands to tear at the thing that assailed him. The red bird, the Jewel bearer, born of my blood from my father's hand, had returned, to defend me.

I let go the rock and advanced upon him, drawing my blade as I went. Brand struck the bird and it flapped away, gaining altitude, circling for another dive. He raised both arms to cover his face and head, but not before I saw the blood that flowed from his left eye socket.

He began to fade again even as I rushed toward him. But the bird descended like a bomb and its talons struck Brand about the head once again. Then the bird, too, began to fade. Brand was reaching for his ruddy assailant and being slashed by it as they both disappeared.

When I reached the place of the action the only thing that remained was the fallen crossbow, and I smashed it with my boot.

Not yet, not yet the end, damn it! How long will you

plague me, brother? How far must I go to bring it to an end between us?

I climbed back down to the trail. Star was not yet dead and I had to finish the job. Sometimes I think I'm in the wrong business.

7

A bowl of cotton candy.

Having traversed the pass, I regarded the valley that lay before me. At least, I assumed that it was a valley. I could see nothing below its cover of cloud/mist/fog.

In the sky, one of the red streaks was turning yellow; another, green. I was slightly heartened by this, as the sky had behaved in a somewhat similar fashion when I had visited the edge of things, across from the Courts of Chaos.

I hitched up my pack and began hiking down the trail. The winds diminished as I went. Distantly, I heard some thunder from the storm I was fleeing. I wondered where Brand had gone. I had a feeling that I would not be seeing him again for a time.

Partway down, with the fog just beginning to creep and curl about me, I spotted an ancient tree and cut myself a staff. The tree seemed to shriek as I severed its limb.

"Damn you!" came something like a voice from within it.

"You're sentient?" I said. "I'm sorry . . ."

"I spent a long time growing that branch. I suppose you are going to burn it now?"

"No," I said. "I needed a staff. I've a long walk before me."

"Through this valley?"

"That's right."

"Come closer, that I may better sense your presence. There is something about you that glows."

I took a step forward.

"Oberon!" it said. "I know thy Jewel."

"Not Oberon," I said. "I am his son. I wear it on his mission, though."

"Then take my limb, and have my blessing with it. I've sheltered your father on many a strange day. He planted me, you see."

"Really? Planting a tree is one of the few things I never saw Dad do."

"I am no ordinary tree. He placed me here to mark a boundary."

"Of what sort?"

"I am the end of Chaos and of Order, depending upon how you view me. I mark a division. Beyond me other rules apply."

"What rules?"

"Who can say? Not I. I am only a growing tower of sentient lumber. My staff may comfort you, however. Planted, it may blossom in strange climes. Then again, it may not. Who can say? Bear it with you, however, son of Oberon, into the place where you journey now. I feel a storm approaching. Good-bye."

"Good-bye," I said. "Thank you."

I turned and walked on down the trail into the deepening fog. The pinkness was drained from it as I went. I shook my head as I thought about the tree, but its staff proved useful for the next several hundred meters, where the going was particularly rough.

Then things cleared a bit. Rocks, a stagnant pool, some small, dreary trees festooned with ropes of moss, a smell of decay . . . I hurried by. A dark bird was watching me from one of the trees.

It took wing as I regarded it, flapping in a leisurely fashion in my direction. Recent events having left me a little bird-shy, I drew back as it circled my head. But then it fluttered to rest on the trail before me, cocked its head and viewed me with its left eye.

"Yes," it announced then. "You are the one."

"The one what?" I said.

"The one I will accompany. You've no objection to a bird of ill omen following you, have you, Corwin?"

It chuckled then, and executed a little dance.

"Offhand, I do not see how I can stop you. How is it that you know my name?"

"I've been waiting for you since the beginning of Time, Corwin."

"Must have been a bit tiresome."

"It has not been all that long, in this place. Time is what you make of it."

I resumed walking. I passed the bird and kept going. Moments later, it flashed by me and landed atop a rock off to my right.

"My name is Hugi," he stated. "You are carrying a piece of old Ygg, I see."

"Ygg?"

"The stuffy old tree who waits at the entrance to this place and won't let anyone rest on his branches. I'll bet he yelled when you whacked it off." He emitted peals of laughter then.

"He was quite decent about it."

"I'll bet. But then, he hadn't much choice once you'd done it. Fat lot of good it will do you."

"It's doing me fine," I said, swinging it lightly in his direction.

He fluttered away from it.

"Hey! That was not funny!"

I laughed.

"I thought it was."

I walked on by.

For a long while, I made my way through a marshy area. An occasional gust of wind would clear the way nearby. Then I would pass it, or the fogs would shift over it once again. Occasionally, I seemed to hear a snatch of music—from what direction, I could not tell—slow, and somewhat stately, produced by a steel-stringed instrument.

As I slogged along, I was hailed from somewhere to my left:

"Stranger! Halt and regard me!"

Wary, I halted. Couldn't see a damned thing through that fog, though.

"Hello," I said. "Where are you?"

Just then, the fogs broke for a moment and I beheld a huge head, eyes on a level with my own. They belonged to what seemed a giant body, sunk up to the shoulders in a quag. The head was bald, the skin pale as milk, with a stony texture to it. The dark eyes probably seemed even darker than they really were by way of contrast.

"I see," I said then. "You are in a bit of a fix. Can you free your arms?"

"If I strain mightily," came the reply.

"Well, let me check about for something stable you can grab onto. You ought to have a pretty good reach there."

"No. That is not necessary."

"Don't you want to get out? I thought that was why you hollered."

"Oh, no. I simply wanted you to regard me."

I moved nearer and stared, for the fog was beginning to shift again.

"All right," I said. "I have seen you."

"Do you feel my plight?"

"Not particularly, if you will not help yourself or accept help."

"What good would it do me to free myself?"

"It is your question. You answer it."

I turned to go.

"Wait! Where do you travel?"

"South, to appear in a morality play."

Just then, Hugi flew out of the fog and landed atop the head. He pecked at it and laughed.

"Don't waste your time, Corwin. There is much less here than meets the eye," he said.

The giant lips shaped my name. Then: "He is indeed the one?"

"That's him, all right," Hugi replied.

"Listen, Corwin," said the sunken giant. "You are going to try to stop the Chaos, aren't you?"

"Yes."

"Do not do it. It is not worth it. I want things to end. I desire a release from this condition."

"I already offered to help you out. You turned me down."

"Not that sort of release. An end to the whole works."

"That is easily done," I said. "Just duck your head and take a deep breath."

"It is not only personal termination that I desire, but an end to the whole foolish game."

"I believe there are a few other folks around who would rather make their own decisions on the matter."

"Let it end for them, too. There will come a time when they are in my position and will feel the same way."

"Then they will possess the same option. Good day."

I turned and walked on.

"You will, too!" he called after me.

As I hiked along, Hugi caught up with me and perched on the end of my staff.

"It's neat to sit on old Ygg's limb now he can't— Yikes!" Hugi sprang into the air and circled.

"Burned my foot! How'd he do that?" he cried.

I laughed.

"Beats me."

He fluttered for a few moments, then made for my right shoulder.

"Okay if I rest here?"

"Go ahead."

"Thanks." He settled. "The Head is really a mental basket case, you know."

I shrugged my shoulders and he spread his wings for balance.

"He is groping after something," he went on, "but proceeding incorrectly by holding the world responsible for his own failings."

"No. He would not even grope to get out of the mud," I said.

"I meant philosophically."

"Oh, that sort of mud. Too bad."

"The whole problem lies with the self, the ego, and its involvement with the world on the one hand and the Absolute on the other."

"Oh, is that so?"

"Yes. You see, we are hatched and we drift on the surface of events. Sometimes, we feel that we actually influence things, and this gives rise to striving. This is a big mistake, because it creates desires and builds up a false ego when just being should be enough. That leads to more desires and more striving and there you are, trapped."

"In the mud?"

"So to speak. One needs to fix one's vision firmly on the Absolute and learn to ignore the mirages, the illusions, the fake sense of identity which sets one apart as a false island of consciousness."

"I had a fake identity once. It helped me a lot in becoming the absolute that I am now—me."

"No, that's fake, too."

"Then the me that may exist tomorrow will thank me for it, as I do that other."

"You are missing the point. That you will be fake, too."

"Why?"

"Because it will still be full of those desires and strivings that set you apart from the Absolute."

"What is wrong with that?"

"You remain alone in a world of strangers, the world of phenomena."

"I like being alone. I am quite fond of myself. I like phenomena, too."

"Yet the Absolute will always be there, calling to you, causing unrest."

"Good, then there is no need to hurry. But yes, I see what you mean. It takes the form of ideals. Everyone has a few. If you are saying that I should pursue them, I agree with you."

"No, they are distortions of the Absolute, and what you are talking about is more striving."

"That is correct."

"I can see that you have a lot to unlearn."

"If you are talking about my vulgar instinct for survival, forget it."

The trail had been leading upward, and we came now to a smooth, level place, almost paved-seeming, though strewn lightly with sand. The music had grown louder and continued to do so as I advanced. Then, through the fog, I saw dim shapes moving, slowly, rhythmically. It took several moments for me to realize that they were dancing to the music.

I kept moving until I could view the figures—human-seeming, handsome folk, garbed in courtly attire—treading to the slow measures of invisible musicians. It was an intricate and lovely dance that they executed, and I halted to watch some of it.

"What is the occasion," I asked Hugi, "for a party out here in the middle of nowhere?"

"They dance," he said, "to celebrate your passage. They are not mortals, but the spirits of Time. They began this foolish show when you entered the valley."

"Spirits?"

"Yes. Observe."

He left my shoulder, flew above them and defecated. The dropping passed through several dancers as if they were holograms, without staining a brocaded sleeve or a silken shirt, without causing any of the smiling figures to miss a measure. Hugi cawed several times then and flew back to me.

"That was hardly necessary," I said. "It is a fine performance."

"Decadent," he said, "and you should hardly take it as a compliment, for they anticipate your failure. They but wish to get in a final celebration before the show is closed."

I watched for a time anyway, leaning upon my staff, resting. The figure described by the dancers slowly shifted, until one of the women—an auburn-haired beauty —was quite near to me. Now, none of the dancers' eyes at any time met my own. It was as if I were not present. But that woman, in a perfectly timed gesture, cast with her right hand something which landed at my feet.

I stooped and found it substantial. It was a silver rose— my own emblem—that I held. I straightened and fixed it at the collar of my cloak. Hugi looked the other way and said nothing. I had no hat to doff, but I did bow to the lady. There might have been a slight twitch at her right eye as I turned to go.

The ground lost its smoothness as I walked, and finally the music faded. The trail grew rougher, and whenever the fogs cleared the only views were of rocks or barren plains. I drew strength from the Jewel when I would otherwise have collapsed, and I noted that each such fix was of shorter duration now.

After a time, I grew hungry and I halted to eat what rations I had left.

Hugi stood on the ground nearby and watched me eat.

"I will admit to a certain small admiration for your persistence," he said, "and even for what you implied when you spoke of ideals. But that is about it. Earlier, we were talking about the futility of desire and of striving—"

"You were. It is not a major concern in my life."

"It should be."

"I have had a long life, Hugi. You insult me by assuming I have never considered these footnotes to sophomore philosophy. The fact that you find consensus reality barren tells me more about you than it does about that state of affairs. To wit, if you believe what you say I feel sorry for you, in that you must for some inexplicable reason be here desiring and striving to influence this false ego of mine rather than free of such nonsense and on your way to your Absolute. If you do not believe it, then it tells me that you have been set to hinder and discourage me, in which case you are wasting your time."

Hugi made a gargling noise. Then: "You are not so blind that you deny the Absolute, the beginning and end of everything?"

"It is not indispensable to a liberal education."

"You admit the possibility?"

"Perhaps I know it better than you, bird. The ego, as I see it, exists at an intermediate stage between rationality and reflex existence. Blotting it out is a retreat, though. If you come from that Absolute—of a self-canceling All—why do you wish to go back home? Do you so despise yourself that you fear mirrors? Why not make the trip worthwhile? Develop. Learn. Live. If you have been sent on a journey why do you wish to cop out and run back to your point of departure? Or did your Absolute make a mistake in sending something of your caliber? Admit that possibility and that is the end of the news."

Hugi glared at me, then sprang into the air and flew off. Going to consult his manual, perhaps. . . .

I heard a peal of thunder as I rose to my feet. I began walking. I had to try to keep ahead of things.

The trail narrowed and widened a number of times before it vanished completely, leaving me to wander across a gravelly plain. I felt more and more depressed as I traveled, trying to keep my mental compass set in the proper direction. I almost came to welcome the sounds of the storm, for they at least gave me a rough idea as to which way was north. Of course, things were a bit confusing in the fog, so that I could not be absolutely certain. And they were growing louder. . . . Damn.

. . . And I had been grieved by the loss of Star, troubled by Hugi's futilitarianism. This was definitely not a good day. I began to doubt that I was going to complete my journey. If some nameless denizen of this dark place did not ambush me before too long, there was a strong possibility that I would wander here until my strength failed or the storm caught me. I did not know whether I would be able to beat back that canceling storm another time. I began to doubt it.

I tried using the Jewel to disperse the fog, but its effects seemed blunted. By my own sluggishness, perhaps. I could clear a small area, but my rate of travel quickly bore me through it. My sense of Shadow was dulled in this place which seemed in some way the essence of Shadow.

Sad. It would have been nice to go out with opera—in a big Wagnerian finale beneath strange skies, against worthy opponents—not scrabbling about in a foggy wasteland.

I passed a familiar-seeming outcrop of stone. Could I have been moving in a circle? There is a tendency to do that when completely lost. I listened for the thunder, to take my bearings again. Perversely, all was silent. I moved to the outcrop and seated myself on the ground, resting my back against it. No sense to merely wandering. I would wait a time for the thunder's signal. I withdrew my Trumps as I sat there. Dad had said that they would

be out of commission for a time, but I had nothing better
to do.

One by one, I went through them all, trying to reach
everyone, save for Brand and Caine. Nothing. Dad had
been right. The cards lacked the familiar coldness. I
shuffled the entire deck then and cast my fortune, there
on the sand. I got an impossible reading and put them all
away again. I leaned back and wished I had some water
left. For a long while, I listened for the storm. There were
a few growls, but they were directionless. The Trumps
made me think of my family. They were up ahead—
wherever that might be—waiting for me. Waiting for
what? I was transporting the Jewel. To what end? At first,
I had assumed that its powers might be necessary in the
conflict. If so, and if I were indeed the only one who
could employ them, then we were in bad shape. I thought
of Amber then, and I was shaken with remorse and a kind
of dread. Things must not end for Amber, ever. There
had to be a way to roll back the Chaos. . . .

I threw away a small stone I had been toying with.
Once I released it, it moved very slowly.

The Jewel. Its slowdown effect again . . .

I drew more energy and the stone shot away. It seemed
that I had just taken strength from the Jewel a little while
ago. While this treatment energized my body, my mind
still felt fogged up. I needed sleep—with lots of rapid eye
movements. This place might seem a lot less unusual if I
were rested.

How close was I to my destination? Was it just beyond
the next mountain range, or an enormous distance farther? And what chance had I of staying ahead of that
storm, no matter what the distance? And the others? Supposing the battle was already concluded and we had lost?

I had visions of arriving too late, to serve only as grave-digger. . . . Bones and soliloquies, Chaos . . .

And where was that damned black road now that I finally had a use for it? If I could locate it, I could follow it. I had a feeling that it was somewhere off to my left. . . .

I reached out once again, parting the fogs, rolling them back. . . . Nothing . . .

A shape? Something moving?

It was an animal, a large dog perhaps, moving to remain within the fog. Was it stalking me?

The Jewel began to pulse as I moved the fog even farther back. Exposed, the animal seemed to shrug itself. Then it moved straight toward me.

8

I stood as it came near. I could see then that it was a jackal, a big one, its eyes fixed on my own.

"You are a little early," I said. "I was only resting."

It chuckled.

"I have come merely to regard a Prince of Amber," the beast said. "Anything else would be a bonus."

It chuckled again. So did I.

"Then feast your eyes. Anything else, and you will find that I have rested sufficiently."

"Nay, nay," said the jackal. "I am a fan of the House of Amber. And that of Chaos. Royal blood appeals to me, Prince of Chaos. And conflict."

"You have awarded me an unfamiliar title. My connection with the Courts of Chaos is mainly a matter of genealogy."

"I think of the images of Amber passing through the shadows of Chaos. I think of the waves of Chaos washing over the images of Amber. Yet at the heart of the order Amber represents moves a family most chaotic, just as the House of Chaos is serene and placid. Yet you have your ties, as well as your conflicts."

"At the moment," I said, "I am not interested in paradox hunting and terminology games. I am trying to get to the Courts of Chaos. Do you know the way?"

"Yes," said the jackal. "It is not far, as the carrion bird flies. Come, I will set you in the proper direction."

It turned and began walking away. I followed.

"Do I move too fast? You seem tired."

"No. Keep going. It is beyond this valley certainly, is it not?"

"Yes. There is a tunnel."

I followed it, out across sand and gravel and dry, hard ground. There was nothing growing at either hand. As we walked, the fogs thinned and took on a greenish cast—another trick of that stippled sky, I assumed.

After a time, I called out, "How much farther is it?"

"Not too far now," it said. "Do you grow tired? Do you wish to rest?"

It looked back as it spoke. The greenish light gave to its ugly features an even more ghastly cast. Still, I needed a guide; and we were heading uphill, which seemed to be proper.

"Is there water anywhere near about?" I asked.

"No. We would have to backtrack a considerable distance."

"Forget it. I haven't the time."

It shrugged and chuckled and walked on. The fog cleared a little more as we went, and I could see that we were entering a low range of hills. I leaned on my staff and kept up the pace.

We climbed steadily for perhaps half an hour, the ground growing stonier, the angle of ascent steeper. I found myself beginning to breathe heavily.

"Wait," I called to him. "I do want to rest now. I thought you said that it was not far."

"Forgive me," it said, halting, "for jackalocentrism. I was judging in terms of my own natural pace. I erred in this, but we *are* almost there now. It lies among the rocks just ahead. Why not rest there?"

"All right," I replied, and I resumed walking.

Soon we reached a stony wall which I realized was the foot of a mountain. We picked our way among the rocky debris which lined it and came at last to an opening which led back into darkness.

"There you have it," said the jackal. "The way is straight, and there are no troublesome side branches. Take your passage through, and good speed to you."

"Thank you," I said, giving up thoughts of rest for the moment and stepping inside. "I appreciate this."

"My pleasure," he said from behind me.

I took several more steps and something crunched beneath my feet and rattled when kicked aside. It was a sound one does not readily forget. The floor was strewn with bones.

There came a soft, quick sound from behind me, and I knew that I did not have time to draw Grayswandir. So I spun, raising my staff before me and thrusting with it.

This maneuver blocked the beast's leap, striking it on the shoulder. But it also knocked me over backward, to roll among the bones. The staff was torn from my hands by the impact, and in the split second of decision allowed me by my opponent's own fall I chose to draw Grayswandir rather than grope after it.

I managed to get my blade unsheathed, but that was all. I was still on my back with the point of my weapon to my left when the jackal recovered and leaped again. I swung the pommel with all of my strength into its face.

The shock ran down my arm and up into my shoulder. The jackal's head snapped back and its body twisted to my left. I brought the point into line immediately, gripping the hilt with both hands, and I was able to rise to my right knee before it snarled and lunged once more.

As soon as I saw that I had it on target, I threw my weight behind it, driving the blade deep into the jackal's body. I released it quickly and rolled away from those snapping jaws.

The jackal shrieked, struggled to rise, dropped back. I lay panting where I had fallen. I felt the staff beneath me and seized it. I brought it around to guard and drew myself back against the cave wall. The beast did not rise again, however, but lay there thrashing. In the dim light, I could see that it was vomiting. The smell was overpowering.

Then it turned its eyes in my direction and lay still.

"It would have been so fine," it said softly, "to eat a Prince of Amber. I always wondered—about royal blood."

Then the eyes closed and the breathing stopped and I was left with the stink.

I rose, back still against the wall, staff still before me, and regarded it. It was a long while before I could bring myself to retrieve my blade.

A quick exploration showed me that I was in no tunnel, but only a cave. When I made my way out, the fog had grown yellow, and it was stirred now by a breeze from the lower reaches of the valley.

I leaned against the rock and tried to decide which way to take. There was no real trail here.

Finally, I struck off to my left. That way seemed somewhat steeper, and I wanted to get above the fog and into the mountains as soon as I could. The staff continued to serve me well. I kept listening for the sound of running water, but there was none about.

I struggled along, always continuing upward, and the

fogs thinned and changed color. Finally, I could see that I was climbing toward a wide plateau. Above it, I began to catch glimpses of the sky, many-colored and churning.

There were several sharp claps of thunder at my back, but I still could not see the disposition of the storm. I increased my pace then, but began to grow dizzy after a few minutes. I stopped and seated myself on the ground, panting. I was overwhelmed with a sense of failure. Even if I made it up to the plateau, I had a feeling that the storm would roar right across it. I rubbed my eyes with the heels of my hands. What was the use of going on if there was no way I could make it?

A shadow moved through the pistachio mists, dropped toward me. I raised my staff, then saw that it was only Hugi. He braked himself and landed at my feet.

"Corwin," he said, "you have come a good distance."

"But maybe not good enough," I said. "The storm seems to be getting nearer."

"I believe that it is. I have been meditating and would like to give you the benefit of—"

"If you want to benefit me at all," I said, "I could tell you what to do."

"What is that?"

"Fly back and see how far off the storm really is, and how fast it seems to be moving. Then come and tell me."

Hugi hopped from one foot to the other. Then, "All right," he said, and leaped into the air and batted his way toward what I felt to be the northwest.

I leaned on the staff and rose. I might as well keep climbing at the best pace I could manage. I drew upon the Jewel again, and strength came into me like a red lightning flash.

As I mounted the slope, a damp breeze sprang up from

the direction in which Hugi had departed. There came another thunderclap. No more growls and rumbles.

I made the most of the influx of energy, climbing quickly and efficiently for several hundred meters. If I were going to lose, I might as well make it to the top first. I might as well see where I was and learn whether there was anything at all left for me to try.

My view of the sky grew more and more clear as I climbed. It had changed considerably since last I had regarded it. Half of it was of uninterrupted blackness and the other half those masses of swimming colors. And the entire heavenly bowl seemed to be rotating about a point directly overhead. I began to grow excited. This was the sky I was seeking, the sky which had covered me that time I had journeyed to Chaos. I struggled higher. I wanted to utter something heartening, but my throat was too dry.

As I neared the rim of the plateau, I heard a flapping sound and Hugi was suddenly on my shoulder.

"The storm is about ready to crawl up your arse," he said. "Be here any minute."

I continued climbing, reached level ground and hauled myself up to it. I stood for a moment then, breathing heavily. The wind must have kept the area clear of fog, for it was a high, smooth plain, and I could see the sky for a great distance ahead. I advanced, to find a point from which I could see beyond the farther edge. As I moved, the sounds of the storm came to me more clearly.

"I do not believe you will make it across," Hugi said, "without getting wet."

"You know that is no ordinary storm," I croaked. "If it were, I'd be thankful for the chance of getting a drink."

"I know. I was speaking figuratively."

I growled something vulgar and kept going.

Gradually, the vista before me enlarged. The sky still did its crazy veil dance, but the illumination was more than sufficient. When I reached a position where I was positive what lay before me, I halted and sagged against my staff.

"What is the matter?" Hugi asked.

But I could not speak. I simply gestured at the great wasteland which commenced somewhere below the farther lip of the plateau to sweep on for at least forty miles before butting up against another range of mountains. And far off to the left and still running strong went the black road.

"The waste?" he said. "I could have told you it was there. Why didn't you ask me?"

I made a noise halfway between a groan and a sob and sank slowly to the ground.

How long I remained so, I am not certain. I felt more than a little delirious. In the midst of it I seemed to see a possible answer, though something within me rebelled against it. I was finally roused by the noises of the storm and Hugi's chattering.

"I can't beat it across that place," I whispered. "There is no way."

"You say you have failed," Hugi said. "But this is not so. There is neither failure nor victory in striving. It is all but an illusion of the ego."

I rose slowly to my knees.

"I did not say that I had failed."

"You said that you cannot go on to your destination."

I looked back, to where lightnings now flashed as the storm climbed toward me.

"That's right, I cannot do it that way. But if Dad

failed, I have got to attempt something that Brand tried to convince me only he could do. I have to create a new Pattern, and I have to do it right here."

"You? Create a new Pattern? If Oberon failed, how could a man who can barely stay on his feet do it? No, Corwin. Resignation is the greatest virtue you might cultivate."

I raised my head and lowered the staff to the ground. Hugi fluttered down to stand beside it and I regarded him.

"You do not want to believe any of the things that I said, do you?" I told him. "It does not matter, though. The conflict between our views is irreducible. I see desire as hidden identity and striving as its growth. You do not." I moved my hands forward and rested them on my knees. "If for you the greatest good is union with the Absolute, then why do you not fly to join it now, in the form of the all-pervading Chaos which approaches? If I fail here, it will become Absolute. As for me, I must try, for so long as there is breath within me, to raise up a Pattern against it. I do this because I am what I am, and I am the man who could have been king in Amber."

Hugi lowered his head.

"I'll see you eat crow first," he said, and he chuckled.

I reached out quickly and twisted his head off, wishing that I had time to build a fire. Though he made it look like a sacrifice, it is difficult to say to whom the moral victory belonged, since I was planning on doing it anyway.

9

. . . Cassis, and the smell of the chestnut blossoms. All along the Champs-Elysées the chestnuts were foaming white. . . .

I remembered the play of the fountains in the Place de la Concorde. . . . And down the Rue de la Seine and along the quais, the smell of the old books, the smell of the river. . . . The smell of chestnut blossoms . . .

Why should I suddenly remember 1905 and Paris on the shadow Earth, save that I was very happy that year and I might, reflexively, have sought an antidote for the present? Yes . . .

White absinthe, Amer Picon, grenadine . . . Wild strawberries, with Crème d'Isigny . . . Chess at the Café de la Régence with actors from the Comédie Française, just across the way . . . The races at Chantilly . . . Evenings at the Boîte à Fursy on the Rue Pigalle . . .

I placed my left foot firmly before my right, my right before my left. In my left hand, I held the chain from which the Jewel depended—and I carried it high, so that I could stare into the stone's depths, seeing and feeling there the emergence of the new Pattern which I described with each step. I had screwed my staff into the ground and left it to stand near the Pattern's beginning. Left . . .

The wind sang about me and there was thunder near at

hand. I did not meet with the physical resistance that I did on the old Pattern. There was no resistance at all. Instead—and in many ways worse—a peculiar deliberation had come over all my movements, slowing them, ritualizing them. I seemed to expend more energy in preparing for each step—perceiving it, realizing it and ordering my mind for its execution—than I did in the physical performance of the act. Yet the slowness seemed to require itself, was exacted of me by some unknown agency which determined precision and an adagio tempo for all my movements. Right . . .

. . . And, as the Pattern in Rebma had helped to restore my faded memories, so this one I was now striving to create stirred and elicited the smell of the chestnut trees, of the wagonloads of vegetables moving through the dawn toward the Halles. . . . I was not in love with anyone in particular at the time, though there were many girls—Yvettes and Mimis and Simones, their faces merge—and it was spring in Paris, with Gipsy bands and cocktails at Louis'. . . . I remembered, and my heart leaped with a kind of Proustian joy while Time tolled about me like a bell. . . . And perhaps this was the reason for the recollection, for this joy seemed transmitted to my movements, informed my perceptions, empowered my will. . . .

I saw the next step and I took it. . . . I had been around once now, creating the perimeter of my Pattern. At my back, I could feel the storm. It must have mounted to the plateau's rim. The sky was darkening, the storm blotting the swinging, swimming, colored lights. Flashes of lightning splayed about, and I could not spare the energy and the attention to try to control things.

Having gone completely around, I could see that as much of the new Pattern as I had walked was now in-

scribed in the rock and glowing palely, bluely. Yet, there
were no sparks, no tingles in my feet, no hair-raising cur-
rents—only the steady law of deliberation, upon me like a
great weight. . . . Left . . .

. . . Poppies, poppies and cornflowers and tall poplars
along country roads, the taste of Normandy cider . . .
And in town again, the smell of the chestnut blossoms
. . . The Seine full of stars . . . The smell of the old brick
houses in the Place des Vosges after a morning's rain . . .
The bar under the Olympia Music Hall . . . A fight there
. . . Bloodied knuckles, bandaged by a girl who took me
home . . . What was her name? Chestnut blossoms . . . A
white rose . . .

I sniffed then. The odor was all but gone from the
remains of the rose at my collar. Surprising that any of it
had survived this far. It heartened me. I pushed ahead,
curving gently to my right. From the corner of my eye, I
saw the advancing wall of the storm, slick as glass, oblit-
erating everything it passed. The roar of its thunder was
deafening now.

Right, left . . .

The advance of the armies of the night . . . Would my
Pattern hold against it? I wished that I might hurry, but
if anything I was moving with increasing slowness as I
went on. I felt a curious sense of bilocation, almost as if I
were within the Jewel tracing the Pattern there myself
while I moved out here, regarding it and mimicking its
progress. Left . . . Turn . . . Right . . . The storm was
indeed advancing. Soon it would reach old Hugi's bones.
I smelled the moisture and the ozone and wondered
about the strange dark bird who had said he'd been waiting for me since the beginning of Time. Waiting to argue
with me or to be eaten by me in this place without his-

tory? Whatever, considering the exaggeration usual in moralists, it was fitting that, having failed to leave me with my heart all laden with rue over my spiritual condition, he be consumed to the accompaniment of theatrical thunder. . . . There was distant thunder, near thunder and more thunder now. As I turned in that direction once more, the lightning flashes were nearly blinding. I clutched my chain and took another step. . . .

The storm pushed right up to the edge of my Pattern, and then it parted. It began to creep around me. Not a drop fell upon me or the Pattern. But slowly, gradually, we came to be totally engulfed within it.

It seemed as if I were in a bubble at the bottom of a stormy sea. Walls of water encircled me and dark shapes darted by. It seemed as if the entire universe were pressing in to crush me. I concentrated on the red world of the Jewel. Left . . .

The chestnut blossoms . . . A cup of hot chocolate at a sidewalk café . . . A band concert in the Tuileries Gardens, the sounds climbing through the sunbright air . . . Berlin in the twenties, the Pacific in the thirties—there had been pleasures there, but of a different order. It may not be the true past, but images of the past that rush to comfort or torment us later, man or nation. No matter. Across the Pont Neuf and down the Rue Rivoli, buses and fiacres . . . Painters at their easels in the Luxembourg Gardens . . . If all were to fall well, I might seek a shadow like this again one day . . . It ranked with my Avalon. I had forgotten . . . The details . . . The touches that make for life . . . The smell of the chestnuts . . .

Walking . . . I completed another circuit. The wind screamed and the storm roared on, but I was untouched. So long as I did not permit it to distract me, so long as I

kept moving and maintained my focus on the Jewel. . . .
I had to hold up, had to keep taking these slow, careful
steps, never to stop, slower and slower but constantly
moving. . . . Faces . . . It seemed that rows of faces
regarded me from beyond the Pattern's edge. . . . Large,
like the Head, but twisted—grinning, jeering, mocking
me, waiting for me to stop or step wrongly. . . . Waiting
for the whole thing to come apart around me. . . . There
was lightning behind their eyes and in their mouths, their
laughter was the thunder. . . . Shadows crawled among
them. . . . Now they spoke to me, with words like a gale
from off a dark ocean. . . . I would fail, they told me, fail
and be swept away, this fragment of a Pattern dashed to
pieces behind me and consumed. . . . They cursed me,
they spat and vomited toward me, though none of it
reached. . . . Perhaps they were not really there. . . .
Perhaps my mind had been broken by the strain. . . .
Then what good were my efforts? A new Pattern to be
shaped by a madman? I wavered, and they took up the
chorus, "Mad! Mad! Mad!" in the voices of the elements.

I drew a deep breath and smelled what was left of the
rose and thought of chestnuts once again, and days filled
with the joys of life and organic order. The voices seemed
to soften as my mind raced back through the events of
that happy year. . . . And I took another step. . . . And
another. . . . They had been playing on my weaknesses,
they could feel my doubts, my anxiety, my fatigue. . . .
Whatever they were, they seized what they saw and tried
to use it against me. . . . Left . . . Right . . . Now let
them feel my confidence and wither, I told myself. I have
come this far. I will continue. Left . . .

They swirled and swelled about me, still mouthing dis-
couragements. But some of the force seemed gone out of

them. I made my way through another section of arc, seeing it grow before me in my mind's red eye.

I thought back to my escape from Greenwood, to my tricking Flora out of information, to my encounter with Random, our fight with his pursuers, our journey back to Amber. . . . I thought of our flight to Rebma and my walking of the reversed Pattern there for a restoration of much of my memory. . . . Of Random's shotgun wedding and my sojourn to Amber, where I fought with Eric and fled to Bleys. . . . Of the battles that followed, my blinding, my recovery, my escape, my journey to Lorraine and then to Avalon. . . .

Moving into even higher gear, my mind skimmed the surface of subsequent events. . . . Ganelon and Lorraine . . . The creatures of the Black Circle . . . Benedict's arm . . . Dara . . . The return of Brand and his stabbing . . . My stabbing . . . Bill Roth . . . Hospital records . . . My accident . . .

. . . Now, from the very beginning at Greenwood, through it all, to this moment of my struggle to assure each perfect maneuver as it appeared to me, I felt the growing sense of anticipation I had known—whether my actions were directed toward the throne, vengeance, or my conception of duty—felt it, was aware of its continuous existence across those years up until this moment, when it was finally accompanied by something else. . . . I felt that the waiting was just about over, that whatever I had been anticipating and struggling toward was soon to occur.

Left . . . Very, very slowly . . . Nothing else was important. I threw all of my will into the movements now. My concentration became total. Whatever lay beyond the Pattern, I was now oblivious to it. Lightnings, faces,

winds . . . It did not matter. There was only the Jewel,
the growing Pattern and myself—and I was barely aware
of myself. Perhaps this was the closest I would ever come
to Hugi's ideal of merging with the Absolute. Turn . . .
Right foot . . . Turn again . . .

Time ceased to have meaning. Space was restricted to
the design I was creating. I drew strength from the Jewel
without summoning it now, as part of the process in
which I was engaged. In a sense, I suppose, I was obliter-
ated. I became a moving point, programed by the Jewel,
performing an operation which absorbed me so totally
that I had no attention available for self-consciousness.
Yet, at some level, I realized that I was a part of the process, also. For I knew, somehow, that if anyone else were
doing it, it would be a different Pattern emerging.

I was vaguely aware that I had passed the halfway
point. The way had become trickier, my movements even
slower. Despite the matter of velocity, I was somehow
reminded of my experiences on originally becoming attuned to the Jewel, in that strange, many-dimensional
matrix which seemed to be the source of the Pattern itself.

Right . . . Left . . .

There was no drag. I felt very light, despite the deliberation. A boundless energy seemed to wash constantly
through me. All of the sounds about me had merged into
a white noise and vanished.

Suddenly then, I no longer seemed to be moving
slowly. It did not seem as if I had passed a Veil or barrier,
but rather that I had undergone some internal adjust-
ment.

It felt as if I were moving at a more normal pace now,
winding my way through tighter and tighter coils, ap-

proaching what would soon be the design's terminus. Mainly, I was still emotionless, though I knew intellectually that at some level a sense of elation was growing and would soon burst through. Another step . . . Another . . . Perhaps half a dozen more paces . . .

Suddenly, the world went dark. It seemed that I stood within a great void, with only the faint light of the Jewel before me and the glow of the Pattern like a spiral nebula through which I was striding. I wavered, but only for an instant. This must be the last trial, the final assault. I would have to be sufficient to the distraction.

The Jewel showed me what to do and the Pattern showed me where to do it. The only thing missing was a view of myself. Left . . .

I continued, executing each move with all of my attention. An opposing force began to rise against me finally, as on the old Pattern. But for this, I was prepared by years of experience. I struggled for two more steps against the mounting barrier.

Then, within the Jewel, I saw the ending of the Pattern. I would have gasped at the sudden realization of its beauty, but at this point even my breath was regulated by my efforts. I threw all of my strength into the next step, and the void seemed to shake about me. I completed it, and the next was even more difficult. I felt as if I were at the center of the universe, treading on stars, struggling to impart some essential motion by what was basically an act of will.

My foot slowly advanced, though I could not see it. The Pattern began to brighten. Soon its blaze was almost blinding.

Just a little farther . . . I strove harder than I ever had on the old Pattern, for now the resistance seemed absolute. I had to oppose it with a firmness and constancy of will that excluded everything else, though I seemed not to be moving at all now, though all of my energies seemed diverted into the brightening of the design. At least, I would go out with a splendid backdrop. . . .

Minutes, days, years . . . I do not know how long this went on. It felt like forever, as if I had been engaged in this single act for all of eternity. . . .

Then I moved, and how long that took I do not know. But I completed the step and began another. Then another . . .

The universe seemed to reel about me. I was through. The pressure was gone. The blackness was gone. . . .

For an instant, I stood at the center of my Pattern. Without even regarding it, I fell forward onto my knees and bent double, my blood pounding in my ears. Head swimming, I panted. I began to shake, all over. I had done it, I realized dimly. Come whatever may, there was a Pattern. And it would endure. . . .

I heard a sound where there should have been none, but my jaded muscles refused to respond, even reflexively, until it was too late. Not until the Jewel was jerked from my limp fingers did I raise my head and roll back onto my haunches. No one had been following me through the Pattern—I was certain that I would have been aware of it. Therefore . . .

The light was almost normal, and blinking against it, I looked up into Brand's smiling face. He wore a black eyepatch now, and he held the Jewel in his hand. He must have teleported himself in.

He struck me just as I raised my head, and I fell onto my left side. He kicked me in the stomach then, hard.

"Well, you've done it," he said. "I did not think you

could. Now I have another Pattern to destroy before I set things right. I need this to turn the battle at the Courts first, though." He waved the Jewel. "Good-bye for now."

And he vanished.

I lay there gasping and clutching at my stomach. Waves of blackness rose and fell, like a surf, within me, though I did not completely succumb to unconsciousness. A feeling of enormous despair washed over me, and I closed my eyes and moaned. There was no Jewel for me to draw upon now, either.

The chestnut trees . . .

10

As I lay there hurting, I had visions of Brand appearing on the battlefield where the forces of Amber and Chaos fought, the Jewel pulsing about his neck. Apparently his control over it was sufficient, as he saw it, to enable him to turn things against us. I saw him lashing out with lightning bolts among our troops. I saw him summoning great winds and hailstorms to strike at us. I almost wept. All of this, when he could still redeem himself by coming in on our side. Just winning was not enough for him now, though. He had to win for himself, and on his own terms. And I? I had failed. I had thrown up a Pattern against the Chaos, a thing I had never thought I could do. Yet, this would be as nothing if the battle was lost and Brand returned and wiped out my work. To have come this close, passing through everything that I had, and then to fail here. . . . It made me want to cry "Injustice!" though I knew the universe did not run in accordance with my notions of equity. I gnashed my teeth and spat some dirt I had mouthed. I had been charged by our father to take the Jewel to the place of battle. I had almost made it.

A sense of strangeness came over me then. Something was calling for my attention. What?

The silence.

The raging winds and the thunder had ceased. The air

was still. In fact, the air felt cool and fresh. And on the other side of my eyelids, I knew that there was light.

I opened my eyes. I saw a sky of a bright, uniform white. I blinked, I turned my head. There was something off to my right. . . .

A tree. A tree stood where I had planted the staff I had cut from old Ygg. It was already far taller than the staff itself had been. I could almost see it growing. And it was green with leaves and white with a sprinkling of buds; a few blossoms had opened. From that direction, the breeze brought me a faint and delicate scent which offered me some comfort.

I felt along my sides. I did not seem to have any broken ribs, though my guts still felt knotted from the kick I had taken. I rubbed my eyes with my knuckles and ran my hands through my hair. I sighed heavily then and rose to one knee.

Turning my head, I regarded the prospect. The plateau was the same, yet somehow not the same. It was still bare but was no longer harsh. Likely an effect of the new illumination. No, there was more to it than that. . . .

I had continued to turn, completing my scanning of the horizon. It was not the same place where I had commenced my walk. There were differences both subtle and gross: altered rock formations, a dip where there had been a rise, a new texture to the stone beneath and near me, in the distance what appeared to be soil. I stood and it seemed that now, from somewhere, I caught the scent of the sea. This place had an entirely different feeling to it than the one to which I had mounted—so long ago, it seemed. It was too much of a change for that storm to have wrought. It reminded me of something.

I sighed again, there at the Pattern's center, and continued to consider my surroundings. Somehow, in spite of myself, my despair was slipping away and a feeling of— "refreshment"—seems somehow the best word—was rising within me. The air was so clean and sweet, and the place had a new, unused feeling about it. I—

Of course. It was like the place of the primal Pattern. I turned back to the tree and regarded it again, higher already. Like, yet unlike . . . There was something new in the air, the ground, the sky. This was a new place. A new primal Pattern. Everything about me then was a result of the Pattern in which I stood.

I suddenly realized that I was feeling more than refreshment. It was now a sense of elation, a kind of joy that was moving through me. This was a clean, fresh place and I was somehow responsible for it.

Time passed. I just stood there watching the trees, looking around me, enjoying the euphoria that had come over me. Here was some kind of victory, anyway—until Brand came back to wipe it out.

Suddenly, I was sober again. I had to stop Brand, I had to protect this place. I was at the center of a Pattern. If this one behaved like the other, I could use its power to project me anywhere I desired. I could use it to go and join the others now.

I dusted myself off. I loosened my blade in the scabbard. Things might not be as hopeless as they had seemed earlier. I had been told to convey the Jewel to the place of battle. So Brand had done it for me; it would still be there. I would simply have to go and take it back from him, somehow, to make things turn the way they were supposed to have fallen.

I looked all around me. I would have to return here, to investigate this new situation at another time, if I sur-

vived what was to come. There was mystery here. It hung
in the air and drifted on the breeze. It could take ages to
unravel what had occurred when I had drawn the new
Pattern.

I saluted the tree. It seemed to stir as I did so. I
adjusted my rose and pushed it back into shape. It was
time to move again. There was a thing I had yet to do.

I lowered my head and closed my eyes. I tried to recall
the lay of the land before the final abyss at the Courts of
Chaos. I saw it then, beneath that wild sky, and I peopled
it with my relatives, with troops. I seemed to hear the
sounds of a distant battle as I did this. The scene adjusted
itself, came clearer. I held the vision an instant longer,
then charged the Pattern to take me there.

. . . A moment later, it seemed, I stood upon a hilltop
beside a plain, a cold wind whipping my cloak about me.
The sky was that crazy, turning, stippled thing I remembered from last time—half-black, half-psychedelic rain-
bows. There were unpleasant fumes in the air. The black
road was off to the right now, crossing that plain and
passing beyond it over the abyss toward that nighted citadel, firefly gleams flickering about it. Gauzy bridges
drifted in the air, extending from far in that darkness, and
strange forms traveled upon them as well as upon the
black road. Below me on the field was what seemed to be
the main concentration of troops. At my back, I heard
something other than Time's winged chariot.

Turning toward what must have been north by a succession of previous reckonings regarding its course, I beheld the advance of that devil-storm through distant
mountains, flashing and growling, coming on like a sky-
high glacier.

So I had not stopped it with the creation of a new Pattern. It seemed that it had simply passed by my protected area and would continue until it got to wherever it was going. Hopefully then, the thing would be succeeded by whatever constructive impulses were now spreading outward from the new Pattern, with the reimposition of order throughout the places of Shadow. I wondered how long it would take for the storm to get here.

I heard the sound of hoofs and turned, drawing my blade. . . .

A horned rider on a great black horse was bearing down upon me, something like firelight glowing in his eyes.

I adjusted my position and waited. He seemed to have descended from one of the gauzy roadways which had drifted in this direction. We were both fairly far removed from the main scene of action. I watched as he mounted the hill. Good horse, that. Nice chest. Where the hell was Brand? I wasn't looking for just any fight.

I watched the rider as he came on, and the crooked blade in his right hand. I repositioned myself as he moved in to cut me down. When he swung, I was ready with a parry that pulled his arm within reach. I caught hold of it and dragged him from his mount.

"That rose . . ." he said as he fell to the ground. I do not know what else he might have said, because I cut his throat, and his words and everything else about him were lost with the fiery slash.

I whirled then, drawing Grayswandir away, sprinted several paces and had hold of the black charger's bridle. I spoke with the horse to calm him and led him away from the flames. After a couple of minutes we were on better terms, and I mounted.

He was skittish at first, but I just had him pace the hill-

top lightly while I continued to observe. The forces of
Amber appeared to be on the offense. Smoldering corpses
were all over the field. The main force of our enemies was
drawn back onto a height near the lip of the abyss. Lines
of them, not yet broken but hard pressed, were falling
back slowly toward it. On the other hand, more troops
were crossing that abyss and joining the others who held
the heights. Estimating their growing numbers and their
position quickly, I judged that these might be readying
an offense of their own. Brand was nowhere in sight.

Even if I had been rested and wearing armor I would
have had second thoughts about riding down and joining
in the fray. My job right now was to locate Brand. I
doubted that he would be directly involved in the
fighting. I looked off to the sides of the battle proper,
seeking a lone figure. No . . . Perhaps the far side of the
field. I would have to circle to the north. There was too
much that I could not see to the west.

I turned my mount and made my way down the hill. It
would be so pleasant to collapse, I decided. Just to fall
down in a heap and sleep. I sighed. Where the hell was
Brand?

I reached the bottom of the hill and turned to cut
through a culvert. I needed a better view—

"Lord Corwin of Amber!"

He was waiting for me as I rounded a bend in the
depression, a big, corpse-colored guy with red hair and a
horse to match. He wore coppery armor with greenish
tracings, and he sat facing me, still as a statue.

"I saw you on the hilltop," he said. "You are not
mailed, are you?"

I slapped my chest.

He nodded sharply. Then he reached up, first to his left

shoulder, then to his right, then to his sides, opening fastenings upon his breastplate. When he had them undone, he removed it, lowered it toward the ground on his left side and let it fall. He did the same with his greaves.

"I have long wanted to meet you," he said. "I am Borel. I do not want it said that I took unfair advantage of you when I killed you."

Borel . . . The name was familiar. Then I remembered. He had Dara's respect and affection. He had been her fencing teacher, a master of the blade. Stupid, though, I saw. He had forfeited my respect by removing his armor. Battle is not a game, and I had no desire to make myself available to any presumptuous ass who thought otherwise. Especially a skilled ass, when I was feeling beat. If nothing else, he could probably wear me down.

"Now we shall resolve a matter which has long troubled me," he said.

I replied with a quaint vulgarism, wheeled my black and raced back the way I had come. He gave chase immediately.

As I passed back along the culvert, I realized that I did not have a sufficient lead. He would be upon me in a matter of moments with my back all exposed, to cut me down or force me to fight. However, while limited, my choices included a little more than that.

"Coward!" he cried. "You flee combat! Is this the great warrior of whom I have heard so much?"

I reached up and unfastened my cloak. At either hand, the culvert's lip was level with my shoulders, then my waist.

I rolled out of the saddle to my left, stumbled once and found my footing. The black went on. I moved to my right, facing the draw.

Catching my cloak in both hands, I swung it in a re-verse-veronica maneuver a second or two before Borel's head and shoulders came abreast of me. It swept over him, drawn blade and all, muffling his head and slowing his arms.

I kicked then, hard. I was aiming for his head, but I caught him on the left shoulder. He was spilled from his saddle, and his horse, too, went by.

Drawing Grayswandir, I leaped after him. I caught him just as he had brushed my cloak aside and was struggling to rise. I skewered him where he sat and saw the startled expression on his face as the wound began to flame.

"Oh, basely done!" he cried. "I had hoped for better of thee!"

"This isn't exactly the Olympic Games," I said, brushing some sparks from my cloak.

I chased down my horse then and mounted. This took me several minutes. As I continued northward, I achieved higher ground. From there, I spotted Benedict directing the battle, and in a draw far to the rear, I caught a glimpse of Julian at the head of his troops from Arden. Benedict was apparently holding them in reserve.

I kept going, toward the advancing storm, beneath the half-dark, half-painted, revolving sky. I soon reached my goal, the highest hill in sight, and began to mount it. I halted several times on the way up, to look back.

I saw Deirdre in black armor, swinging an ax; Llewella and Flora were among the archers. Fiona was nowhere in sight. Gérard was not there either. Then I saw Random on horseback, swinging a heavy blade, leading an assault toward the enemy's high ground. Near him was a knight clad in green whom I did not recognize. The man swung a mace with deadly efficiency. He wore a bow upon his back, and he'd a quiver of gleaming arrows at his hip.

The sounds of the storm came louder as I reached the summit of my hill. The lightning flickered with the regularity of a neon tube and the rain sizzled down, a fiberglass curtain that had now passed over the mountains.

Below me, both beasts and men—and more than a few beast-men—were woven in knots and strands of battle. A cloud of dust hung over the field. Assessing the distribution of forces, however, it did not appear to me that the growing forces of the enemy could be pushed much farther. In fact, it seemed that it was just about time for the counterattack. They appeared to be ready up in their craggy places, and just waiting for the order.

I was about a minute and a half off. They advanced, sweeping down the slope, reinforcing their lines, pushing our troops back, driving ahead. And more were arriving from beyond the dark abyss. Our own troops began a reasonably orderly retreat. The enemy pressed harder, and when things seemed about ready to be turned into a rout an order must have been given.

I heard the sound of Julian's horn, and shortly thereafter I saw him astride Morgenstern leading the men of Arden onto the field. This balanced the opposing forces almost exactly and the noise level rose and rose while the sky turned above us.

I watched the conflict for perhaps a quarter of an hour, as our own forces slowly withdrew across the field. Then I saw a one-armed figure on a fiery striped horse suddenly appear atop a distant hill. He bore a raised blade in his hand and he was faced away from me, toward the west.

He stood unmoving for several long moments. Then he lowered the blade.

I heard trumpets in the west, and at first I saw nothing. Then a line of cavalry came into view. I started. For a moment, I thought Brand was there. Then I realized it was Bleys leading his troops to strike at the enemy's exposed flank.

And suddenly, our troops in the field were no longer retreating. They were holding their line. Then, they were pressing forward.

Bleys and his riders came on, and I realized that Benedict had the day again. The enemy was about to be ground to pieces.

Then a cold wind swept over me from out of the north, and I looked that way again.

The storm had advanced considerably. It must have started moving faster just recently. And it was darker now than it had been, with brighter flashes and louder roars. And this cold, wet wind was increasing in intensity.

I wondered then . . . would it simply sweep over the field like an annihilating wave and that be that? What of the effects of the new Pattern? Would these follow, to restore everything? Somehow, I doubted this. If this storm smashed us, I'd a feeling we would stay smashed. It would require the force of the Jewel to permit us to ride it out until order was restored. And what would be left if we survived it? I simply could not guess.

So what was Brand's plan? What was he waiting for? What was he going to do?

I looked out over the battlefield once more. . . .

Something.

In a shadowy place on the heights where the enemy

had regrouped, been reinforced, and down which it had stormed . . . something.

A tiny flash of red . . . I was sure I had seen it.

I kept watching, waiting. I had to see it again, to pinpoint it. . . .

A minute passed. Two, perhaps . . .

There! And again.

I wheeled the black charger. It looked possible to make it around the enemy's near flank and up to that supposedly vacant height. I raced down the hill and began that course.

It had to be Brand with the Jewel. He had chosen a good, safe spot, from which he commanded a view of the entire battlefield as well as the approaching storm. From there, he could direct its lightning into our troops as the front advanced. He would signal a retreat at the proper moment, hit us with the storm's strange furies, then sidetrack the thing to bypass the side he was backing. It seemed the simplest and most effective use of the Jewel under the circumstances.

I would have to get close fast. My control of the stone was greater than his, but it diminished with distance, and he would have the Jewel on his person. My best bet would be to charge right into him, to get within control range at all costs, take over command of the stone and use it against him. But he might have a bodyguard up there with him. That troubled me, because dealing with it could slow me disastrously. And if he did not, what was to prevent him from teleporting himself away if the going got too rough? Then what could I do? I would have to start all over, hunting him again. I wondered whether I could use the Jewel to keep him from transporting himself. I did not know. I resolved to try.

It might not have been the best of plans, but it was the only one I had. There was no longer time to plot.

As I rode, I saw that there were others headed for that height, also. Random, Deirdre and Fiona, mounted and accompanied by eight horsemen, had made their way through the enemy lines, with a few other troops—friends or foes, I could not tell—maybe both—riding hard behind them. The knight clad in green seemed to be moving the fastest, gaining on them. I did not recognize him—or her, as the case might be. I did not doubt the objective of the vanguard, however—not with Fiona there. She must have detected Brand's presence and be leading the others to him. A few drops of hope fell upon my heart. She might be able to neutralize Brand's powers, or minimize them. I leaned forward, still bearing to my left, hurrying my horse along. The sky kept turning. The wind whistled about me. A terrific clap of thunder rolled by. I did not look back.

I was racing them. I did not want them to get there before me, but I feared that they would. The distance was just too great.

If only they would turn and see me coming, they would probably wait. I wished there had been some way of giving them a sign of my presence earlier. I cursed the fact that the Trumps no longer worked.

I began shouting. I screamed after them, but the wind blew my words away and the thunder rolled over them.

"Wait for me! Damn it! It's Corwin!"

Not even a glance in my direction.

I passed the nearest engagements and rode along the enemy's flank out of range of missiles and arrows. They seemed to be retreating faster now and our troops were spreading out over a larger area. Brand must be getting ready to strike. Part of the rotating sky was covered by a dark cloud which had not been above the field minutes before.

I turned toward my right, behind the retreating forces, racing on toward those hills the others were already mounting.

The sky continued to darken as I neared the foot of the hills, and I feared for my kinsmen. They were getting too close to him. He would have to do something. Unless Fiona was strong enough to stop him. . . .

The horse reared and I was thrown to the ground at the blinding flash which had occurred before me. The thunder cracked before I hit the earth.

I lay there for several moments, dazed. The horse had run off, was perhaps fifty meters away, before he halted and began to move about uncertainly. I rolled onto my stomach and looked up the long slope. The other riders were also down. Their group had apparently been struck by the discharge. Several were moving, more were not. None had yet risen. Above them, I saw the red glow of the Jewel, back beneath an underhang, brighter and steadier now, and the shadowy outline of the figure who wore it.

I began crawling forward, upward and to my left. I wanted to get out of line of sight with that figure before I risked rising. It would take too long to reach him crawling, and I was going to have to skirt the others now, because his attention would be with them.

I made my way carefully, slowly, using every bit of cover in sight, wondering whether the lightning would be striking in the same place again soon—and if not, when he would begin pulling disaster down upon our troops. Any minute now, I judged. A glance back showed me our forces spread over the far end of the field, with the enemy pulled back and coming this way. Before too long, in fact, it seemed I might have them to worry about, too.

I made it into a narrow ditch and wormed my way south for perhaps ten meters. Out again then on the far side, to take advantage of a rise, then some rocks.

When I raised my head to take stock of the situation, I could no longer see the glow of the Jewel. The cleft from which it had shone was blocked by its own eastern shoulder of stone.

I kept crawling, though, near to the lip of the great abyss itself, before I bore to my right once more. I reached a point where it seemed safe to rise, and I did so. I kept expecting another flash, another thunderclap— nearby or on the field—but none came. I began to wonder . . . why not? I reached out, trying to sense the presence of the Jewel, but I could not. I hurried toward the place where I had seen the glow.

I glanced back over the abyss to be sure that no new menaces were approaching from that direction. I drew my blade. When I reached my goal, I stayed close to the escarpment and worked my way northward. I dropped low when I came to its edge and peered around.

There was no red glow. No shadowy figure either. The stony recess appeared to be empty. There was nothing suspicious anywhere in the vicinity. Could he have teleported again? And if so, why?

I rose and passed about the rocky rise. I continued moving in that direction. I tried once more to feel the Jewel, and this time I made a faint contact with it— somewhere off to my right and above, it seemed.

Silent, wary, I moved that way. Why had he left his

shelter? He had been perfectly situated for what he had been about. Unless . . .

I heard a scream and a curse. Two different voices. I began to run.

11

I passed the niche and kept going. Beyond it, there was a natural trail winding upward. I mounted this.

I could see no one as yet, but my sense of the Jewel's presence grew stronger as I moved. I thought that I heard a single footfall from off to my right and I whirled in that direction, but there was no one in sight. The Jewel did not feel that near either, so I continued.

As I neared the top of the rise, the black drop of Chaos hanging behind, I heard voices. I could not distinguish what was being said, but the words were agitated.

I slowed as I neared the crest, lowered myself and peered around the side of a rock.

Random was a small distance ahead of me and Fiona was with him, as were Lords Chantris and Feldane. All, save Fiona, held weapons as if ready to use them, but they stood perfectly still. They were staring toward the edge of things—a shelf of rock slightly above their level and perhaps fifteen meters distant—the place where the abyss began.

Brand stood in that place, and he was holding Deirdre before him. She was unhelmed, her hair blowing wild, and he had a dagger at her throat. It appeared that he had already cut her slightly. I dropped back.

I heard Random say softly, "Is there nothing more you can do, Fi?"

"I can hold him here," she said, "and at this range, I can slow his efforts at weather control. But that is all. He's got some attunement with it and I do not. He also has proximity going for him. Anything else I might try, he can counter."

Random gnawed his lower lip.

"Put down your weapons," Brand called out. "Do it now, or Deirdre's dead."

"Kill her," Random said, "and you lose the only thing that's keeping you alive. Do it, and I'll show you where I'll put my weapon."

Brand muttered something under his breath. Then: "Okay. I will start by mutilating her."

Random spat.

"Come on!" he said. "She can regenerate as well as the rest of us. Find a threat that means something, or shut up and fight it out!"

Brand was still. I thought it better not to reveal my presence. There must be something I could do. I ventured another look, mentally photographing the terrain before I dropped back. There were some rocks way off to the left, but they did not extend far enough. I saw no way that I might sneak up on him.

"I think we are going to have to rush him and chance it," I heard Random say. "I don't see anything else. Do you?"

Before anyone answered him, a strange thing occurred. The day began to grow brighter.

I looked all about me for the source of the illumination, then sought it overhead.

The clouds were still there, the crazy sky doing its tricks beyond them. The brightness was in the clouds, however. They had paled and were now glowing, as if they masked a sun. Even as I watched, there was a perceptible brightening.

"What is he up to now?" Chantris asked.

"Nothing that I can tell," Fiona said. "I do not believe it is his doing."

"Whose then?"

There was no answer that I could overhear.

I watched the clouds grow brighter. The largest and brightest of them seemed to swirl then, as if stirred. Forms tossed within it, settled. An outline began to take shape.

Below me, on the field, the sounds of battle lessened. The storm itself was muted as the vision grew. Something was definitely forming in the bright place above our heads—the lines of an enormous face.

"I do not know, I tell you," I heard Fiona say in response to something mumbled.

Before it finished taking form, I realized that it was my father's face in the sky. Neat trick, that. And I had no idea what it represented either.

The face moved, as if he were regarding us all. There were lines of strain there, and something of concern to his expression. The brightness grew a little further. His lips moved.

When his voice came down to me it was somehow at an ordinary conversational level, rather than the vast booming I had expected:

"I send you this message," he said, "before undertaking the repair of the Pattern. By the time you receive it, I will already have succeeded or failed. It will precede the wave of Chaos which must accompany my endeavor. I have reason to believe the effort will prove fatal to me."

His eyes seemed to sweep across the field.

"Rejoice or mourn, as you would," he went on, "for this is either the beginning or the end. I will send the Jewel of Judgment to Corwin as soon as I have finished with it. I have charged him to bear it to the place of conflict. All of your efforts there will be as nothing if the wave of Chaos cannot be averted. But with the Jewel, in that place, Corwin should be able to preserve you until it passes."

I heard Brand's laugh. He sounded quite mad now.

"With my passing," the voice continued, "the problem of the succession will be upon you. I had wishes in this regard, but I see now that these were futile. Therefore, I have no choice but to leave this on the horn of the Unicorn.

"My children, I cannot say that I am entirely pleased with you, but I suppose this works both ways. Let it be. I leave you with my blessing, which is more than a formality. I go now to walk the Pattern. Good-bye."

Then his face began to fade and the brightness drained out of the cloudbank. A little while, and it was gone. A stillness lay upon the field.

". . . and, as you can see," I heard Brand saying, "Corwin does not have the Jewel. Throw down your weapons and get the hell out of here. Or keep them and get out. I do not care. Leave me alone. I have things to do."

"Brand," Fiona said, "can you do what he wanted of Corwin? Can you use it to make that thing miss us?"

"I could if I would," he said. "Yes, I could turn it aside."

"You will be a hero if you do," she said gently. "You will earn our gratitude. All past wrongs will be forgiven. Forgiven and forgotten. We—"

He began to laugh wildly.

"*You* forgive *me?*" he said. "You, who left me in that

tower, who put the knife into my side? Thank you, sister. It is very kind of you to offer to forgive me, but excuse me if I decline."

"All right," Random said, "what *do* you want? An apology? Riches and treasure? An important appointment? All of these? They are yours. But this is a stupid game you are playing. Let us end it and go home, pretend it was all a bad dream."

"Yes, let us end it," Brand replied. "You do that by throwing down your weapons first. Then Fiona releases me from her spell, you all do an about-face and march north. You do it or I kill Deirdre."

"Then I think you had better go ahead and kill her and be ready to fight it out with me," he said, "because she will be dead in a little while anyway, if we let you have your way. All of us will."

I heard Brand's chuckle.

"Do you honestly think I am going to let you die? I need you—as many of you as I can save. Hopefully Deirdre, too. You are the only ones who can appreciate my triumph. I will preserve you through the holocaust that is about to begin."

"I do not believe you," Random said.

"Then take a moment and think about it. You know me well enough to know that I will want to rub your noses in it. I want you as witnesses to what I do. In this sense, I require your presence in my new world. Now, get out of here."

"You will have everything you want plus our gratitude," Fiona began, "if you will just—"

"Go!"

I knew that I could delay no longer. I had to make my move. I also knew that I could not reach him in time. I had no choice but to try using the Jewel as a weapon against him.

I reached out and felt its presence. I closed my eyes and summoned my powers.

Hot. Hot, I thought. It is burning you, Brand. It is causing every molecule in your body to vibrate faster and faster. You are about to become a human torch—

I heard him scream.

"Corwin!" he bellowed. "Stop it! Wherever you are! I'll kill her! Look!"

Still willing the Jewel to burn him, I rose to my feet. I glared at him across the distance that separated us. His clothing was beginning to smolder.

"Stop it!" he cried, and he raised the knife and slashed Deirdre's face.

I screamed and my eyes swam. I lost control of the Jewel. But Deirdre, her left cheek bloody, sank her teeth into his hand as he moved to cut her again. Then her arm was free, and she jabbed her elbow into his ribs and tried to pull away.

As soon as she moved, as soon as her head dropped, there was a silver flash. Brand gasped and let go the dagger. An arrow had pierced his throat. Another followed an instant later and stood out from his breast, a little to the right of the Jewel.

He stepped backward and made a gurgling noise. Only there was no place to which he might step, from the edge of the abyss.

His eye went wide as he began to topple. Then his right hand shot forward and caught hold of Deirdre's hair. I was running by then, shouting, but I knew that I could not reach them in time.

Deirdre howled, a look of terror on her bloodstreaked face, and she reached out to me. . . .

Then Brand, Deirdre and the Jewel were over the edge and falling, vanished from sight, gone. . . .

I believe that I tried to throw myself after them, but Random caught hold of me. Finally, he had to hit me, and it all went away.

When I came around, I lay upon the stony earth farther back from the edge of that place where I had fallen. Someone had folded my cloak into a pillow for me. My first vision was of the turning sky, reminding me somehow of my dream of the wheel the day I had met Dara. I could feel the others about me, hear their voices, but I did not at first turn my head. I just lay there and regarded the mandala in the heavens and thought upon my loss. Deirdre . . . she had meant more to me than all the rest of the family put together. I cannot help it. That is how it was. How many times had I wished she were not my sister. Yet, I had reconciled myself to the realities of our situation. My feelings would never change, but . . . now she was gone, and this thought meant more to me than the impending destruction of the world.

Yet, I had to see what was happening now. With the Jewel gone, everything was over. Yet . . . I reached out, trying to feel its presence, wherever it might be, but there was nothing. I began to rise then, to see how far the wave had advanced, but a sudden arm pushed me back.

"Rest, Corwin." It was Random's voice. "You're beat. You look as if you have just crawled through hell. There is nothing you can do now. Take it easy."

"What difference does the state of my health make?" I replied. "In a little while, it will not matter."

I made to rise again, and this time the arm moved to support me.

"All right, then," he said. "Not that much worth seeing, though."

I suppose that he was right. The fighting appeared to be over except for a few isolated pockets of resistance by the enemy, and these were rapidly being enveloped, their combatants slain or captured, everyone moving in this direction, withdrawing before the advancing wave which had reached the far end of the field. Soon our height would be crowded with all of the survivors from both sides. I looked behind us. No new forces were approaching from the dark citadel. Could we retreat to that place when the wave finally reached us here? Then what? The abyss seemed the ultimate answer. "Soon," I muttered, thinking of Deirdre. "Soon . . ." Why not?

I watched the stormfront, flashing, masking, transforming. Yes, soon. With the Jewel gone along with Brand—

"Brand . . ." I said. "Who was it finally got him?"

"I claim that distinction," said a familiar voice which I could not place.

I turned my head and stared. The man in green was seated on a rock. His bow and quiver lay beside him on the ground. He flashed an evil smile in my direction.

It was Caine.

"I'll be damned," I said, rubbing my jaw. "A funny thing happened to me on the way to your funeral."

"Yes. I heard about it." He laughed. "You ever kill yourself, Corwin?"

"Not recently. How'd you manage it?"

"Walked to the proper shadow," he said, "waylaid the shadow of myself there. He provided the corpse." He shuddered. "An eerie feeling, that. Not one I'd care to repeat."

"But why?" I said. "Why fake your death and try to frame me for it?"

"I wanted to get to the root of the trouble in Amber," he said, "and destroy it. I thought it best to go underground for that. What better way than by convincing everyone that I was dead? I finally succeeded, too, as you saw." He paused. "I'm sorry about Deirdre, though. But I had no choice. It was our last chance. I did not really think he would take her with him."

I looked away.

"I had no choice," he repeated. "I hope you can see that."

I nodded.

"But why did you try to make it look as if I had killed you?" I asked.

Just then Fiona approached with Bleys. I greeted them both and turned back to Caine for my answer. There were things I wanted to ask Bleys, too, but they could wait.

"Well?" I said.

"I wanted you out of the way," he said. "I still thought you might be behind the whole thing. You or Brand. I had it narrowed down that far. I thought it might even be the two of you in it together—especially with him struggling to bring you back."

"You have that wrong," said Bleys. "Brand was trying to keep him away. He had learned that his memory was returning and—"

"I gather," Caine replied, "but at the time it looked that way. So I wanted Corwin back in a dungeon while I searched for Brand. I lay low then and listened in on the

Trumps to everything everyone said, hoping for a clue as to Brand's whereabouts."

"That's what Dad meant," I said.

"What?" Caine asked.

"He implied there was an eavesdropper on the Trumps."

"I do not see how he could have known. I had learned to be completely passive about it. I had taught myself to deal them all out and touch all of them lightly at the same time, waiting for a stirring. When it came, I would shift my attention to the speakers. Taking you one at a time, I even found I could sometimes get into your minds when you were not using the Trumps yourselves—if you were sufficiently distracted and I allowed myself no reaction."

"Yet he knew," I said.

"It is entirely possible. Likely, even," said Fiona, and Bleys nodded.

Random drew nearer.

"What did you mean when you asked about Corwin's side?" he inquired. "How could you even know about it unless—"

Caine merely nodded. I saw Benedict and Julian together in the distance, addressing their troops. At Caine's silent movement, I forgot them.

"You?" I croaked. "You stabbed me?"

"Have a drink, Corwin," Random said, passing me his flask. It was a dilute wine. I gulped it. My thirst was immense, but I stopped after several good swigs.

"Tell me about it," I said.

"All right. I owe you that," he said. "When I learned from Julian's mind that you had brought Brand back to Amber, I decided that an earlier guess had been correct—that you and Brand were in it together. That meant you both had to be destroyed. I used the Pattern to project myself into your chambers that night. There, I tried to kill you, but you moved too fast and you somehow managed to Trump out before I got a second chance."

"Well, damn your eyes," I said. "If you could touch our minds couldn't you have seen that I was not the man you were looking for?"

He shook his head.

"I could pick up only surface thoughts and reactions to your immediate environment. Not always that, even. And I had heard your curse, Corwin. And it was coming true. I could see it all around us. I felt that we would all be a lot safer with you and Brand both out of the way. I knew what he could do, from his actions back before your return. I could not get at him just then, though, because of Gérard. Then he began to grow stronger. I made one effort later, but it failed."

"When was that?" Random asked.

"That was the one Corwin got blamed for. I masked myself. In case he managed to get away as Corwin had, I did not want him knowing I was still around. I used the Pattern to project myself into his chambers and tried to finish him off. We were both hurt—there was a lot of blood around—but he managed to Trump away, too. Then I got in touch with Julian a while back and joined him for this battle, because Brand just had to show up here. I had some silver-tipped arrows made because I was more than half convinced that he was no longer like the rest of us. I wanted to kill him fast and do it from a distance. I practiced my archery and came looking for him. I finally found him. Now everyone tells me I was wrong about you, so I guess your arrow will go unused."

"Thanks a lot."

"I might even owe you an apology."

"That would be nice."

"On the other hand, I thought that I was right. I was doing it to save the rest—"

I never did get Caine's apology, because just then a trumpet blast seemed to shake the entire world—directionless, loud, prolonged. We cast about, seeking its source.

Caine stood and pointed.

"There!" he said.

My eyes followed his gesture. The curtain of the storm-front was broken off to the northwest, at the point where the black road emerged from it. There, a ghostly rider on a black horse had appeared and was winding his horn. It was a while before more of its notes reached us. Moments later, two more trumpeters—also pale, and mounted on black steeds—joined him. They raised their horns and added to the sound.

"What can it be?" Random asked.

"I think I know," Bleys said, and Fiona nodded.

"What, then?" I asked.

But they did not answer me. The horsemen were beginning to move again, passing along the black road, and more were emerging behind them.

12

I watched. There was a great silence on the heights about me. All of the troops had halted and were regarding the procession. Even the prisoners from the Courts, hemmed by steel, turned their attention that way.

Led by the pale trumpeters came a mass of horsemen mounted on white steeds, bearing banners, some of which I did not recognize, behind a man-thing who bore the Unicorn standard of Amber. These were followed by more musicians, some of them playing upon instruments of a sort I had never seen before.

Behind the musicians marched horned man-shaped things in light armor, long columns of them, and every twentieth or so bore a great torch before him, reaching high above his head. A deep noise came to us then—slow, rhythmic, rolling beneath the notes of the trumpets and the sounds of the musicians—and I realized that the foot soldiers were singing. A great deal of time seemed to pass as this body advanced along that black way across the distant track below us, yet none of us stirred and none of us spoke. They passed, with the torches and the banners and the music and the singing, and they finally came to the edge of the abyss and continued over the near-invisible extension of that dark highway, their torches flaring against the blackness now, lighting their way. The music grew stronger, despite the distance, with more and more voices added to that chorus, as the guard continued to emerge from that flashing stormcurtain. An occasional roll of thunder passed by, but this could not drown it; nor did the winds which assailed the torches extinguish any so far as I could see. The movement had a hypnotic effect. It seemed that I had been watching the procession for countless days, years perhaps, listening to the tune I now recognized.

Suddenly, a dragon sailed through the stormfront, and another, and another. Green and golden and black as old iron, I watched them soar on the winds, turning their heads to trail pennons of fire. The lightning flashed behind them and they were awesome and magnificent and of incalculable size. Beneath them came a small herd of white cattle, tossing their heads and blowing, beating the ground with their hoofs. Riders passed beside and among these, cracking long black whips.

Then came a procession of truly bestial troops from a shadow with which Amber sometimes has commerce—heavy, scaled, taloned—playing upon instruments like bagpipes, whose skirling notes came to us with vibrance and pathos.

These marched on, and there were more torch bearers and more troops with their colors—from shadows both distant and near. We watched them pass and wind their way into the far sky, like a migration of fireflies, their destination that black citadel called the Courts of Chaos.

There seemed no end to it. I had lost all track of time. But the stormfront, strangely, was not advancing as all this went on. I had even lost something of my sense of person, to be caught up in the procession which passed us. This, I knew, was an event which could never be repeated. Bright flying things darted above the columns and dark ones floated, higher.

There were ghostly drummers, beings of pure light and a flock of floating machines; I saw horsemen, clad all in black, mounted on a variety of beasts; a wyvern seemed to hang in the sky for a moment, like part of a fireworks display. And the sounds—of hoofbeats and footfalls, of singing and skirling, of drumming and trumpeting—mounted to a mighty wave that washed over us. And on, on, on out over the bridge of darkness, wound the procession, its lights lining the great span for a vast distance now.

Then, as my eyes drifted back along those lines, another shape emerged from the glistening curtain. It was a cart draped all in black and drawn by a team of black horses. At each corner rose a staff which glowed with blue fire, and atop it rested what could only be a casket, draped with our Unicorn flag. The driver was a hunchback clad in purple and orange garments, and I knew even at that distance that it was Dworkin.

It is thus, then, I thought. *I do not know why, but somehow it is fitting, fitting that it be the Old Country to which you travel now. There were many things that I might have said while you lived. Some of them I did say, but few of the right words were ever spoken. Now it is over, for you are dead. As dead as all of those who have gone before you into that place where the rest of us soon may follow. I am sorry. It was only after all these years, on your assuming another face and form, that I finally knew you, respected you, even came to like you—though you were a crochety old bastard in that form, too. Was the Ganelon self the real you all along, or was it only another form adopted for convenience's sake, Old Shape-*

shifter? I will never know, but I like to think that I finally saw you as you were, that I met someone I liked, someone I could trust, and that it was you. I wish that I might have known you even better, but I am grateful for this much. . . .

"Dad . . . ?" Julian said softly.

"He wanted to be taken beyond the Courts of Chaos and into the final darkness when his time came at last," Bleys said. "So Dworkin once told me. Beyond Chaos and Amber, to a place where none reigned."

"And so it is," Fiona said. "But is there order somewhere beyond that wall they come through? Or does the storm go on forever? If he succeeded, it is but a passing matter and we are in no danger. But if he did not . . ."

"It does not matter," I said, "whether or not he succeeded, because I did."

"What do you mean?" she asked.

"I believe that he failed," I said, "that he was destroyed before he could repair the old Pattern. When I saw this storm coming—actually, I experienced a part of it —I realized that I could not possibly make it here in time with the Jewel, which he had sent to me after his efforts. Brand had been trying to get it from me all along the way —to create a new Pattern, he said. Later, that gave me the idea. When I saw that all else was failing, I used the Jewel to create a new Pattern. It was the most difficult thing I ever did, but I succeeded. Things should hold together after this wave passes, whether we survive it or not. Brand stole the Jewel from me just as I completed it. When I recovered from his attack I was able to use the new Pattern to project me here. So there is still a Pattern, no matter what else happens."

"But Corwin," she said, "what if Dad succeeded?"

"I do not know."

"It is my understanding," Bleys said, "from things that Dworkin told me, that two distinct Patterns could not exist in the same universe. Those in Rebma and Tir-na Nog'th do not count, being but reflections of our own. . . ."

"What would happen?" I said.

"I think there would be a splitting off, the founding of a new existence—somewhere."

"Then what would its effect be upon our own?"

"Either total catastrophe or no effect whatsoever," Fiona said. "I can make a case for its going either way."

"Then we are right back where we started," I said. "Either things are going to fall apart shortly or they are going to hold."

"So it would seem," Bleys said.

"It does not matter, if we are not going to be around after that wave gets to us," I said. "And it will."

I turned my attention back to the funeral cortege. More horsemen had emerged behind the wagon, followed by marching drummers. Then pennons and torches and a long line of foot soldiers. The singing still came to us, and far, far out over the abyss it seemed the procession might finally have reached that dark citadel.

. . . I hated you for so long, blamed you for so many things. Now it is over, and none of these feelings remain. Instead, you had even wanted me to be king, a job for which—I see now—I am not fitted. I see that I must have meant something to you after all. I will never tell the others. It is enough to know it myself. But I can never think of you in the same fashion again. Already your image blurs. I see Ganelon's face where yours should be. He was my companion. He risked his neck for me. He was

you, but a different you—a you that I had not known. How many wives and enemies had you outlived? Were there many friends? I think not. But there were so many things about you of which we knew nothing. I never thought that I would see your passing. Ganelon—Father— old friend and enemy, I bid you farewell. You join Deirdre, whom I have loved. You have preserved your mystery. Rest in peace, if that be your will. I give you this withered rose I have borne through hell, casting it into the abyss. I leave you the rose and the twisted colors in the sky. I will miss you. . . .

Finally, the long line came to an end. The last marchers emerged from the curtain and moved away. The lightning still flared, the rain still poured and the thunder rumbled. No member of the procession that I could recall had seemed wet, however. I had been standing at the edge of the abyss, watching them pass. There was a hand on my arm. How long it had been there, I could not tell. Now that the passage was complete, I realized that the storm-front was advancing again.

The rotation of the sky seemed to be bringing more darkness upon us. There were voices off to my left. It seemed they had been talking for a long while, but I had not been hearing their words. I realized that I was shaking, that I ached all over, that I could barely stand.

"Come and lie down," Fiona said. "The family has shrunken enough for one day."

I let her lead me away from the edge.

"Would it really make any difference?" I asked. "How much longer do you think we have?"

"We do not have to stay here and wait for it," she said. "We will cross the dark bridge into the Courts. We have already broken their defense. The storm may not reach

that far. It may be stopped here by the abyss. We ought
to see Dad off, anyway."

I nodded.

"It would seem we have small choice but to be dutiful
unto the end."

I eased myself down and sighed. If anything, I felt
even weaker now.

"Your boots . . ." she said.

"Yes."

She pulled them off. My feet throbbed.

"Thanks."

"I'll get you some rations."

I closed my eyes. I dozed. Too many images played
within my head to make for a coherent dream. How long
this lasted, I do not know, but an old reflex drew me to
wakefulness at the sound of an approaching horse. Then a
shadow passed over my eyelids.

I looked up and beheld a muffled rider, silent, still. I
was regarded.

I looked back. No threatening gesture had been made,
but there was a feeling of antipathy in that cold gaze.

"There lies the hero," said a soft voice.

I said nothing.

"I could slay you easily now."

I recognized the voice then, though I had no idea as to
the reason behind the sentiment.

"I came upon Borel before he died," she said. "He told
me how ignobly you had bested him."

I could not help it, I could not control it. A dry chuckle
rose in my throat. Of all the stupid things to get upset
about. I might have told her that Borel had been far better equipped and far fresher than I, and that he had come
to me looking for a fight. I might have told her that I do

not recognize rules when my life is at stake, or that I do not consider war a game. I could have said a great number of things, but if she did not know them already or did not choose to understand them, they would not have made a bit of difference. Besides, her feelings were already plain.

So I simply said one of the great trite truths: "There is generally more than one side to a story."

"I will settle for the one I have," she told me.

I thought about shrugging, but my shoulders were too sore.

"You have cost me two of the most important persons in my life," she said then.

"Oh?" I said. "I'm sorry, for you."

"You are not what I was led to believe. I had seen you as a truly noble figure—strong, yet understanding and sometimes gentle. Honorable . . ."

The storm, much closer now, was flaring at her back. I thought of something vulgar and said it. She let it pass as if she had not heard me.

"I am going now," she said, "back to my own people. You have won the day thus far—but that way lay Amber." She gestured toward the storm. I could only stare. Not at the raging elements. At her. "I doubt there is anything of my new allegiance left for me to renounce," she continued.

"What about Benedict?" I asked softly.

"Don't . . ." she said, and she turned away. There was a silence. Then, "I do not believe that we will ever meet again," she said, and her horse carried her off to my left, in the direction of the black road.

A cynic might have decided that she had simply chosen to toss in her lot with what she now saw as the winning side, as the Courts of Chaos would likely survive. I simply did not know. I could think only of what I had seen when she had gestured. The cowling had slipped away and I had gotten a glimpse of what she had become. It had not been a human face, there within the shadows. But I turned my head and watched until she was gone. With Deirdre, Brand and Dad gone, and now a parting with Dara on these terms, the world was much emptier—whatever was left of it.

I lay back and sighed. Why not just remain here when the others departed, wait for the storm to wash over me, and sleep . . . dissolve? I thought of Hugi. Had I digested his flight from life as well as his flesh? I was so tired that it seemed the easiest course. . . .

"Here, Corwin."

I had been dozing again, though only for a moment. Fiona was beside me once more, with rations and a flask. Someone was with her.

"I did not wish to interrupt your audience," she said. "So I waited."

"You heard?" I asked.

"No, but I can guess," she said, "since she is gone. Here."

I swallowed some wine, turned my attention to the meat, the bread. Despite my state of mind, they tasted good to me.

"We will be moving soon," Fiona said, casting a glance at the raging stormfront. "Can you ride?"

"I think so," I said.

I took another drink of the wine.

"But too much has happened, Fi," I told her. "I have gone numb emotionally. I broke out of a sanitarium on a shadow world. I have tricked people and I've killed people. I have calculated and I have fought. I won back my memory and I have been trying to straighten out my life. I have found my family, and found that I love it. I have been reconciled with Dad. I have fought for the kingdom. I have tried everything I know to hold things together. Now it appears that it has all come to nothing, and I have not enough spirit left to mourn further. I have gone numb. Forgive me."

She kissed me.

"We are not yet beaten. You will be yourself again," she said.

I shook my head.

"It is like the last chapter of *Alice*," I said. "If I shout, 'You are only a pack of cards!' I feel we will all fly into the air, a hand of painted pasteboards. I am not going with you. Leave me here. I am only the Joker, anyway."

"Right now, I am stronger than you are," she said. "You are coming."

"It is not fair," I said softly.

"Finish eating," she said. "There is still some time."

As I did, she went on, "Your son Merlin is waiting to see you. I would like to call him up here now."

"Prisoner?"

"Not exactly. He was not a combatant. He just arrived a little while ago, asking to see you."

I nodded and she went away. I abandoned my rations and took another swig of wine. I had just become nervous. What do you say to a grown son you only recently learned existed? I wondered about his feelings toward me. I wondered whether he knew of Dara's decision. How should I act with him?

I watched him approach from a place where my relatives were clustered, far off to my left. I had wondered why they had left me by myself this way. The more visitors I received the more apparent it became. I wondered whether they were holding up the withdrawal because of me. The storm's moist winds were growing stronger. He was staring at me as he advanced, no special expression on that face so much like my own. I wondered how Dara felt now that her prophecy of the destruction seemed to have been fulfilled. I wondered how her relationship with the boy actually stood. I wondered . . . many things.

He leaned forward to clasp my hand.

"Father . . ." he said.

"Merlin." I looked into his eyes. I rose to my feet, still holding his hand.

"Do not get up."

"It is all right." I clasped him to me, then released him. "I am glad," I said. Then: "Drink with me." I offered him the wine, partly to cover my lack of words.

"Thank you."

He took it, drank some and passed it back.

"Your health," I said and took a sip myself. "Sorry I cannot offer you a chair."

I lowered myself to the ground. He did the same.

"None of the others seemed to know exactly what you have been doing," he said, "except for Fiona, who said only that it had been very difficult."

"No matter," I said. "I am glad to have made it this far, if for no other reason than this. Tell me of yourself, son. What are you like? How has life treated you?"

He looked away.

"I have not lived long enough to have done too much," he said.

I was curious whether he possessed the shapeshifting ability, but restrained myself from asking at this point. No sense in looking for our differences when I had just met him.

"I have no idea what it was like," I said, "growing up in the Courts."

He smiled for the first time.

"And I have no idea what it would have been like anywhere else," he responded. "I was different enough to be left to myself a lot. I was taught the usual things a gentleman should know—magic, weapons, poisons, riding, dancing. I was told that I would one day rule in Amber. This is not true anymore, is it?"

"It does not seem too likely in the foreseeable future," I said.

"Good," he replied. "This is the one thing I did not want to do."

"What do you want to do?"

"I want to walk the Pattern in Amber as Mother did and gain power over Shadow, so that I might walk there and see strange sights and do different things. Do you think I might?"

I took another sip and I passed him the wine.

"It is quite possible," I said, "that Amber no longer exists. It all depends on whether your grandfather succeeded in something he attempted—and he is no longer around to tell us what happened. However, one way or the other, there is a Pattern. If we live through this demon storm, I promise you that I will find you a Pattern, instruct you and see you walking it."

"Thanks," he said. "Now will you tell me of your journey here?"

"Later," I told him. "What did they tell you of me?"

He looked away.

"I was taught to dislike many of the things about

Amber," he finally said. Then, after a pause: "You, I was taught to respect, as my father. But I was reminded that you were of the party of the enemy." Another pause. "I remember that time on patrol, when you had come to this place and I found you, after your fight with Kwan. My feelings were mixed. You had just slain someone I had known, yet—I had to admire the stance you took. I saw my face in your own. It was strange. I wanted to know you better."

The sky had rotated completely and the darkness was now above us, the colors passing over the Courts. The steady advance of the flashing stormfront was emphasized by this. I leaned forward and reached for my boots, began pulling them on. Soon it would be time to begin our retreat.

"We will have to continue our conversation on your home ground," I said. "It is about time to fly the storm."

He turned and considered the elements, then looked back out over the abyss.

"I can summon a filmy if you wish."

"One of those drifting bridges such as you rode on the day we met?"

"Yes," he answered. "They are most convenient. I—"

There had been a shout from the direction of my assembled relatives. Nothing threatening seemed to be about when I regarded them. So I got to my feet and took a few steps toward them, Merlin rising to follow me.

Then I saw her. A white form, pawing air it seemed, and rising out of the abyss. Her front hoofs finally struck its brink, and she came forward and then stood still, regarding us all: our Unicorn.

13

For a moment, my aches and my fatigue fell away. I felt a tiny twinge of something like hope as I considered the dainty white form which stood before us. A part of me wanted to rush forward, but something much stronger kept me motionless, waiting.

How long we stood thus, I could not tell. Below, on the slopes, the troops had been readying themselves for travel. The prisoners had been bound, horses loaded, equipment secured. But this vast army in the process of march ordering its gear had suddenly halted. It was not natural that they should have become aware so quickly, but every head that I could see was turned in this direction, toward the Unicorn on the brink, limned against that wild sky.

I was suddenly aware that the wind at my back had grown still, though the thunder continued to rumble and explode and the lightning flares threw dancing shadows before me.

I thought of the other time I had seen the Unicorn—at the recovery of the Shadow-Caine's body, the day I had lost a fight with Gérard. I thought of the stories I had heard. . . . Could she really help us?

The Unicorn took a step forward and halted.

She was such a lovely thing that somehow I was heartened just by looking upon her. It was a kind of aching feeling that she aroused, though; hers was a beauty of the sort to be taken in small doses. And I could somehow sense the unnatural intelligence within that snowy head. I wanted very badly to touch her, but knew that I could not.

She cast her gaze all about. Her eyes lighted upon me, and I would have looked away if I had been able. This was not possible, however, and I returned that gaze in which I read an understanding beyond my own. It was as if she knew everything about me, and in this instant had comprehended all of my recent trials—seeing, understanding, possibly sympathizing. For a moment, I felt that I saw something of pity and a strong love reflected there— and perhaps a touch of humor.

Then her head turned and the gaze was broken. I sighed involuntarily. At that moment, in the lightning's glare, I thought I caught a glimpse of something shining at the side of her neck.

She advanced another step, and now she was looking upon the crowd of my kinsmen toward which I had been moving. She lowered her head and made a small whickering noise. She tapped at the earth with her right front hoof.

I felt Merlin at my side. I thought upon things I would be losing if it all ended here.

She took several dancing steps forward. She tossed her head and lowered it. It seemed that she did not like the notion of approaching so large a group of people.

At her next step, I saw the glitter again, and more. A tiny spark of red shone through her fur farther down on her neck. She was wearing the Jewel of Judgment. How she had retrieved it, I had no idea. And it did not matter. If she would just deliver it, I felt that I could break the storm—or at least shield us from this section of it until it had passed.

But that one glance had been enough. She paid me no more heed. Slowly, carefully, as if ready to bolt at the slightest disturbance, she advanced upon the spot where Julian, Random, Bleys, Fiona, Llewella, Benedict and several nobles stood.

I should have realized then what was occurring, but I did not. I simply watched the sleek beast's movements as she picked her way forward, passing about the periphery of the group.

She halted once again and lowered her head. Then she shook her mane and dropped to her front knees. The Jewel of Judgment hung suspended from her twisted, golden horn. The tip of her horn was almost touching the person before whom she knelt.

Suddenly, in my mind's eye, I saw our father's face in the heavens, and his words came back to me: "With my passing, the problem of the succession will be upon you. . . . I have no choice but to leave this on the horn of the Unicorn."

A murmur moved through the group, as I realized this same thought must be occurring to the others. The Unicorn did not stir at this disturbance, however, but remained a soft, white statue, not even seeming to breathe.

Slowly, Random reached forward and removed the Jewel from her horn. His whisper carried to me.

"Thank you," he said.

Julian unsheathed his blade and placed it at Random's feet as he knelt. Then Bleys and Benedict and Caine, Fiona and Llewella. I went and joined them. So did my son.

Random stood silent for a long while. Then, "I accept your allegiance," he said. "Now get up, all of you."

As we did, the Unicorn turned and bolted. She raced down the slope and was out of sight in a matter of moments.

"I had never expected anything like this to happen," Random said, still holding the Jewel at eye level. "Corwin, can you take this thing and stop that storm?"

"It is yours now," I said, "and I do not know how extensive the disturbance is. It occurs to me that in my present condition I might not be able to hold up long enough to keep us all safe. I think it is going to have to be your first regal act."

"Then you are going to have to show me how to work it. I thought we needed a Pattern to perform the attunement."

"I think not. Brand indicated that a person who was already attuned could attune another. I have given it some thought since then, and I believe I know how to go about it. Let's get off to one side somewhere."

"Okay. Come on."

Already, something new had come into his voice and posture. The sudden role had begun working its change immediately, it seemed. I wondered what sort of king and queen he and Vialle would become. Too much. My mind felt disassociated. Too much had happened too recently. I could not contain all of the latest events in one big piece of thinking. I just wanted to crawl off somewhere and sleep around the clock. Instead, I followed him to a place where a small cooking fire still smoldered.

He poked at the fire and tossed a handful of sticks onto it. Then he seated himself close to it and nodded to me. I went over and sat down beside him.

"About this king business," he said. "What am I going to do, Corwin? It caught me totally unprepared."

"Do? Probably a very good job," I replied.

"Do you think there were many hard feelings?"

"If there were, they did not show," I said. "You were a good choice, Random. So much has happened recently . . . Dad sheltered us actually, maybe more than was good for us. The throne is obviously no plum. You have a lot of hard work ahead of you. I think the others have come to realize this."

"And yourself?"

"I wanted it only because Eric did. I did not realize it at the time, but it is true. It was the winning counter in a game we had been playing across the years. The end of a vendetta, really. And I would have killed him for it. I am glad now that he found another way to die. We were more alike than we were different, he and I. I did not realize that until much later either. But after his death, I kept finding reasons for not taking the throne. Finally, it dawned on me that it was not really what I wanted. No. You are welcome to it. Rule well, brother. I am sure that you will."

"If Amber still exists," he said after a time, "I will try. Come, let us be about this business with the Jewel. That storm is getting uncomfortably near."

I nodded and took the stone from his fingers. I held it by its chain with the fire behind it. The light came through; its insides seemed clear.

"Lean closer and stare into the Jewel with me," I directed.

He did this, and while we both regarded the stone, I told him, "Think of the Pattern," and I commenced thinking of it myself, trying to summon to mind its loops and swirls, its palely glowing lines.

I seemed to detect a slight flaw near to the stone's center. I considered it as I thought upon the twistings, the turns, the Veils. . . . I imagined the current which swept through me every time I essayed that complex way.

The imperfection in the stone grew more distinct.

I lay my will upon it, summoning it into fullness, clarity. A familiar feeling came over me as this occurred. It was that which had taken me on the day I had attuned myself to the Jewel. I only hoped that I was strong enough now to go through the experience once again.

I reached out and clasped Random by the shoulder.

"What do you see?" I asked him.

"Something like the Pattern," he said, "only it seems to be three dimensional. It lies at the bottom of a red sea. . . ."

"Come with me then," I said. "We must go to it."

Again, that feeling of movement, drifting at first, then falling with increasing velocity toward the never fully seen sinuosities of the Pattern within the Jewel. I willed us ahead, feeling my brother's presence beside me, and the ruby glow which surrounded us darkened, becoming the blackness of a clean night sky. This special Pattern grew with each thudding heartbeat. Somehow, the process seemed easier than it had before—perhaps because I was already attuned.

Feeling Random beside me, I drew him along as that familiar shape grew and its starting point became apparent. As we were moved in that direction, I once again tried to encompass the totality of this Pattern and was lost once more in what seemed its extra-dimensional convolutions. Great curves and spirals and knotted-seeming traceries wound before us. The sense of awe I had felt earlier swept over me, and from somewhere nearby I was aware of this in Random, also.

We progressed to the section of the beginning and were swept into it. There was a shimmering brightness all about us flashed through with sparks as we were woven into the matrix of light. This time, my mind was entirely absorbed by the process and Paris seemed far away. . . .

A subconscious memory reminded me of the more difficult sections, and here I employed my desire—my will, if you like—to hurry us along the dazzling route, recklessly drawing strength from Random to accelerate the process.

It was as if we negotiated the luminous interior of an enormous and elaborately convoluted seashell. Only our passage was soundless, and we ourselves disembodied points of sentience.

Our velocity seemed to increase constantly, as did a mental aching I did not recall from the previous traversal of the design. Perhaps it was related to my fatigue, or to my efforts to hurry things so. We crashed through the barriers; we were surrounded by steady, flowing walls of brightness. I felt myself growing faint, dizzy, now. But I could not afford the luxury of unconsciousness, nor could I permit us to move more slowly with the storm as near as I remembered it. Again, regretfully, I drew strength from Random—this time just to keep us in the game. We sped ahead.

This time, I did not experience the tingling, fiery sensation of somehow being shaped. It must have been an effect of my attunement. My previous passage through it might have rendered me some small immunity in this regard.

After a timeless interval, it seemed that I felt Random falter. Perhaps I represented too great a drain upon his energies. I began to wonder whether I would leave him with sufficient strength to manipulate the storm if I leaned upon him any further. I resolved not to draw upon his resources any more than I already had. We were well along the way. He should be able to continue without me, if it came to that. I would simply have to hang on as best I could now. Better for me to be lost here than both of us.

We swept on, my senses rebelling, the dizziness recurring. I set my will to our progress and forced everything else from my mind. It seemed we were nearing the terminus when a darkening began which I knew was not a part of the experience. I fought down panic.

It was no good. I felt myself slipping away. So close! I was certain we were almost finished. It would be so easy to—

Everything swam away from me. My last sensation was a knowledge of Random's concern.

It was flickering orange and red between my feet. Was I trapped in some astral hell? I continued to stare as my mind slowly cleared. The light was surrounded by darkness and . . .

There were voices, familiar . . .

Things cleared. I was lying on my back, feet toward a campfire.

"It is all right, Corwin. It is all right."

It was Fiona who had spoken. I turned my head. She was seated on the ground above me.

"Random . . . ?" I said.

"He is all right, also—Father."

Merlin was seated off to the right.

"What happened?"

"Random bore you back," Fiona said.

"Did the attunement work?"

"He thinks so."

I struggled to sit up. She tried to push me back, but I sat up anyway.

"Where is he?"

She gestured with her eyes.

I looked and I saw Random. He was standing with his back to us about thirty meters away, on a shelf of rock, facing the storm. It was very close now, and a wind whipped his garments. Lightning trails crissed and crossed before him. The thunder boomed almost constantly.

"How long—has he been there?" I asked.

"Only a few minutes," Fiona replied.

"That is how long it has been—since our return?"

"No," she said. "You have been out for a fairly long while. Random talked with the others first, then ordered a troop withdrawal. Benedict has taken them all to the black road. They are crossing over."

I turned my head.

There was movement along the black road, a dark column heading out toward the citadel. Gossamer strands drifted between us; there were a few sparks at the far end, about the nighted hulk. Overhead, the sky had completely reversed itself, with us beneath the darkened half. Again, I felt that strange feeling of having been here long, long ago, to see that this, rather than Amber, was the true center of creation. I grasped after the ghost of a memory. It vanished.

I searched the lightning-shot gloom about me.

"All of them—gone?" I said to her. "You, me, Merlin, Random—we're the only ones left here?"

"Yes," Fiona said. "Do you wish to follow them now?"

I shook my head.

"I am staying here with Random."

"I knew you would say that."

I got to my feet as she did. So did Merlin. She clapped her hands and a white horse came ambling up to her.

"You have no further need for my ministrations," she said. "So I will go and join the others in the Courts of Chaos. There are horses for you tethered by those rocks." She gestured. "Are you coming, Merlin?"

"I will stay with my father, and the king."

"So be it. I hope to see you there soon."

"Thanks, Fi," I said.

I helped her to mount and watched her ride off.

I went over and sat down by the fire again. I watched Random, who stood unmoving, facing the storm.

"There are plenty of rations and wine," Merlin said. "May I fetch you some?"

"Good idea."

The storm was so close that I could have walked down to it in a couple of minutes. I could not tell yet whether Random's efforts were having any effect. I sighed heavily and let my mind drift.

Over. One way or another, all of my efforts since Greenwood were over. No need for revenge any longer. No. We had an intact Pattern, maybe even two. The cause of all our troubles, Brand, was dead. Any residuum of my curse was bound to be wiped out by the massive convulsions sweeping through Shadow. And I had done my best to make up for it. I had found a friend in my father and come to terms with him as himself before his death. We had a new king, with the apparent blessing of the Unicorn, and we had pledged him our loyalty. It seemed sincere to me. I was reconciled with my entire family. I felt that I had done my duty. Nothing drove me now. I had run out of causes and was as close as I might ever be to peace. With all this behind me, I felt that if I had to die now, it was all right. I would not protest quite so loudly as I would have at any other time.

"You are far from here, Father."

I nodded, then smiled. I accepted some food and began eating. As I did, I watched the storm. Still too early to be certain, but it seemed that it was no longer advancing.

I was too tired to sleep. Or something like that. My aches had all subsided and a wondrous numbness had come over me. I felt as if I were embedded in warm cotton. Events and reminiscences kept the mental clockwork turning within me. It was, in many ways, a delicious feeling.

I finished eating and built up the fire. I sipped the wine and watched the storm, like a frosted window set before a fireworks display. Life felt good. If Random succeeded in pulling this one off, I would be riding into the Courts of Chaos tomorrow. What might await me there, I could not tell. Perhaps it might be a gigantic trap. An ambush. A trick. I dismissed the thought. Somehow, right now, it did not matter.

"You had begun telling me of yourself, Father."

"Had I? I do not recall what I said."

"I would like to get to know you better. Tell me more."

I made a popping noise with my lips and shrugged.

"Then this." He gestured. "This whole conflict. How did it get started? What was your part in it? Fiona told me that you had dwelled in Shadow for many years without your memory. How did you get it back and locate the others, and return to Amber?"

I chuckled. I regarded Random and the storm once more. I took a drink of wine and drew up my cloak against the wind.

"Why not?" I said then. "If you've a stomach for long stories, that is. . . . I suppose that the best place to begin is at Greenwood Private Hospital, on the shadow Earth of my exile. Yes . . ."

14

The sky turned, and turned again as I spoke. Standing
against the storm, Random prevailed. It broke before us,
parting as if cloven by a giant's axblade. It rolled back at
either hand, finally sweeping off to the north and the
south, fading, diminishing, gone. The landscape it had
masked endured, and with it went the black road. Merlin
tells me that this is no problem, though, for he will summon a strand of gossamer when the time comes for us to
cross over.

Random is gone now. The strain upon him was immense. In repose, he no longer looked as once he did—the
brash younger brother we delighted in tormenting—for
there were lines upon his face which I had never noticed
before, signs of some depth to which I had paid no heed.
Perhaps my vision has been colored by recent events, but
he seemed somehow nobler and stronger. Does a new role
work some alchemy? Appointed by the Unicorn,
anointed by the storm, it seems that he had indeed assumed a kingly mien, even in slumber.

I have slept—even as Merlin now dozes—and it pleases
me to be, for this brief while before his awakening, the
only spot of sentience on this crag at the rim of Chaos,
looking back upon a surviving world, a world that has
been scoured, a world which endures. . . .

We may have missed Dad's funeral, his drifting into

some nameless place beyond the Courts. Sad, but I lacked the strength to move. And yet, I have seen the pageant of his passing, and I bear much of his life within me. I have said my good-byes. He would understand. And good-bye, Eric. After all this time I say it, in this way. Had you lived so long, it would have been over between us. We might even one day have become friends, all our causes for strife passed. Of them all, you and I were more alike than any other pair within the family. Save, in some ways, Deirdre and myself. . . . But tears on this count were shed long ago. Good-bye again, though, dearest sister, you will always live somewhere in my heart.

And you Brand . . . With bitterness do I regard your memory, mad brother. You almost destroyed us. You nearly toppled Amber from her lofty perch on the breast of Kolvir. You would have shattered all of Shadow. You almost broke the Pattern and redesigned the universe in your own image. You were mad and evil, and you came so close to realizing your desires that I tremble even now. I am glad that you are gone, that the arrow and the abyss have claimed you, that you sully no more the places of men with your presence nor walk in the sweet airs of Amber. I wish that you had never been born and, failing that, that you had died sooner. Enough! It diminishes me to reflect so. Be dead and trouble my thinking no more.

I deal you out like a hand of cards, my brothers and sisters. It is painful as well as self-indulgent to generalize like this, but you—I—we—seem to have changed, and before I move into the traffic again I require a final look.

Caine, I never liked you and I still do not trust you. You have insulted me, betrayed me and even stabbed me. Forget that. I do not like your methods, though I cannot fault your loyalty this time around. Peace, then. Let the new reign begin with a clean slate between us.

Llewella, you possess reserves of character the recent situation did not call upon you to exercise. For this, I am grateful. It is sometimes pleasant to emerge from a conflict untested.

Bleys, you are still a figure clad in light to me—valiant, exuberant and rash. For the first, my respect, for the second, my smile. And the last seems to have at least been tempered in recent times. Good. Stay away from conspiracies in the future. They do not suit you well.

Fiona, you have changed the most. I must substitute a new feeling for an old one, princess, as we have become for the first time friends. Take my fondness, sorceress. I owe you.

Gérard, slow, faithful brother, perhaps we have not all changed. You stood rock-like and held to what you believed. May you be less easily gulled. May I never wrestle you again. Go down to your sea in your ships and breathe the clean salt air.

Julian, Julian, Julian . . . Is it that I never really knew you? No. Arden's green magic must have softened that old vanity during my long absence, leaving a juster pride and something I would fain call fairness—a thing apart from mercy, to be sure, but an addition to your armory of traits I'll not disparage.

And Benedict, the gods know you grow wiser as time burns its way to entropy, yet you still neglect single examples of the species in your knowledge of people. Perhaps I'll see you smile now this battle's done. Rest, warrior.

Flora . . . Charity, they say, begins at home. You seem no worse now than when I knew you long ago. It is but a sentimental dream to regard you and the others as I do,

totting up my balance sheets, looking for credits. We are
not enemies, any of us, now, and that should be sufficient.

And the man clad in black and silver with a silver rose
upon him? He would like to think that he has learned
something of trust, that he has washed his eyes in some
clear spring, that he has polished an ideal or two. Never
mind. He may still be only a smart-mouthed meddler,
skilled mainly in the minor art of survival, blind as ever
the dungeons knew him to the finer shades of irony.
Never mind, let it go, let it be. I may never be pleased
with him.

Carmen, *voulez-vous venir avec moi?* No? Then good-
bye to you too, Princess of Chaos. It might have been fun.

The sky is turning once more, and who can say what
deeds its stained-glass light might shine upon? The soli-
taire has been dealt and played. Where there had been
nine of us now there are seven and one a king. Yet Merlin
and Martin are with us, new players in the ongoing game.

My strength returns as I stare into the ashes and consider the path I have taken. The way ahead intrigues me,
from hell to hallelujah. I have back my eyes, my memories, my family. And Corwin will always be Corwin, even
on Judgment Day.

Merlin is stirring now, and this is good. It is time to be
about. There are things to do.

Random's last act after defeating the storm was to join
with me, drawing power from the Jewel, to reach Gérard
through his Trump. They are cold once more, the cards,
and the shadows are themselves again. Amber stands.
Years have passed since we departed it, and more may
elapse before I return. The others may already have
Trumped home, as Random has done, to take up his
duties. But I must visit the Courts of Chaos now, because

I said that I would, because I may even be needed there.

We ready our gear now, Merlin and I, and soon he will summon a wispy roadway.

When all is done in that place, and when Merlin has walked his Pattern and gone to claim his worlds, there is a journey that I must make. I must ride to the place where I planted the limb of old Ygg, visit the tree it has grown to. I must see what has become of the Pattern I drew to the sound of pigeons on the Champs-Elysées. If it leads me to another universe, as I now believe it will, I must go there, to see how I have wrought.

The roadway drifts before us, rising to the Courts in the distance. The time has come. We mount and move forward.

We are riding now across the blackness on a road that looks like cheesecloth. Enemy citadel, conquered nation, trap, ancestral home . . . We shall see. There is a faint flickering from battlement and balcony. We may even be in time for a funeral. I straighten my back and I loosen my blade. We will be there before much longer.

Good-bye and hello, as always.